FACING
THE
ENEMY

THE ADVENTURES of Young
JOSEPH WILLIAMS

FACING
THE
ENEMY

— **Dean Hughes** —

REVISED EDITION

DESERET
BOOK

SALT LAKE CITY, UTAH

NORTHERN MISSOURI

1831–1839

Scale in Miles

0	10	20

Grand River

LIVINGSTON

CARROLL

DeWitt ●

Exodus to Illinois
150 Miles Far West to Quincy

SALINE

Columbi ●

PETTIS

For my parents, Emery and Lorraine Hughes

First printing in hardbound 1982
First printing in paperbound 1991
First printing in paperbound, revised edition 2005

Visit us at deseretbook.com

Library of Congress Cataloging-in-Publication Data

Hughes, Dean, 1943-
  Facing the enemy / Dean Hughes.
     p. cm. — (The adventures of young Joseph Williams ; v. 3)
  Summary: Recently settled in the Mormon community of Far West in northern Missouri, sixteen-year-old Joseph Williams begins to fear that the growing hostility of the old settlers towards the Mormons will force them to move again.
  ISBN 1-59038-449-0 (pbk.)
  [1. Mormons—Fiction.   2. Family life—Missouri—Fiction.   3. Frontier and pioneer life—Missouri—Fiction.   4. Missouri—History—19th century—Fiction.]   I. Title.
  PZ7.H87312Fac 2005
  [Fic]—dc22   2005003623

Printed in Canada   29359
Friesens, Manitoba, Canada

10   9   8   7   6   5   4   3   2   1

Chapter 1

Joseph Williams approached the Prophet, but he didn't say anything. Joseph Smith was standing in front of Lightner's store talking to a couple of men. But when he saw young Joseph, he smiled and put out his hand to him. "Joseph Williams, how are you? Look how you've grown this winter!"

"I'm fine," Joseph said, smiling but holding back a little. Joseph Smith was not satisfied with a handshake, however. He pulled the boy close and wrapped his powerful arms around him.

"Brethren, could we be excused for a moment?" the Prophet asked. "I need to talk to this young man." He took Joseph by the arm and walked with him across the street to the Far West town square, where a great hole had been dug for the foundation of the temple. "Joseph, how is your family?"

"We're doing fine, Brother Joseph. We've already paid off our forty acres with the first year's crop."

"Well, that sounds good. When I was here last fall, I saw the fine house you boys built for your mother. I'm proud of the way you've taken hold. I know it hasn't been easy without your father. You know, Joseph, you're proving yourself to be everything I always said you would be."

The Prophet took a few steps closer to the temple excavation and looked in. Joseph thought that he had changed a little. He didn't seem as happy and playful as usual. But there was still a feeling of power about him. It was in his shoulders and arms, and in his voice. "I wish you wouldn't say that about me, Brother Joseph. I'm still not what I ought to be."

"What do you mean?"

"I'm just not very religious, I guess."

Suddenly the Prophet laughed, and Joseph thought he looked more like his old self. "Not religious? What makes you say that, Joseph?"

"Well, I'm just not. I still hate to sit and listen to sermons as much as I ever did."

The Prophet was still smiling, and his eyes seemed to take on the intense blue of the sky. "How old are you?" he asked.

"I'll be sixteen next week."

"Well, I don't know many sixteen-year-old boys who like to sit in church for hours and listen to us old men preach."

"I don't mind hearing *you*, Brother Joseph."

"Well now, that's a good sign." He laughed again. "And surely the Lord will forgive us both if we nod off once in a while when Brother Rigdon gets going and won't quit." He put his hand on the boy's shoulder. "But Joseph, don't tell me that you're not religious. You can't afford to underestimate yourself that way." The Prophet looked at him closely, no longer smiling. "How old were you when your father died?"

"Twelve."

"And your brother couldn't have been more than fourteen." Joseph nodded. "Look what you've done. Look what your mother has done. You could have pulled out and gone back to New York instead of starting all over again out here on this prairie. You could have turned your back on the Church, but you didn't."

Joseph nodded, looking down, and then said, "Mother promised Father that she would stay with the Saints."

"But that's just the point." He waited until Joseph looked at him. "You've kept your promises. Look about you, son, and you'll see many who haven't. Look what Warren Parrish and his band of rascals have done to me in Kirtland. I was lucky to get out of Ohio with my life. And look what's happening right here in Far West with the Whitmers and Oliver Cowdery. Joseph, these brethren were with me from the first. They know the truth. And now they're turning their backs on what they know. The religious ones are not those who love good preaching, but those who keep their promises. Do you understand that?"

Joseph could feel the Prophet's presence, but he didn't like to look at him directly. "I guess I do," he said. "But Matthew's still the righteous one. When he's working on the farm, he's building God's kingdom. That's how he thinks of it. I've tried. I've worked hard since we came here. I've stayed right by Matthew's side. But I don't find the joy in it that he does."

Joseph Smith still had his hand on the boy's shoulder. "No, I don't suppose farming will be your love, though you'll do your share of it. In a couple of years I'll send you out to preach the gospel. How would you like that?"

Joseph grinned. He was wearing no hat, and his blond hair was tangled by the breeze. "I think I'd rather farm," he said.

"Well, I suspect you'll be a better preacher than you think, Joseph. Are you still going to school?"

"Yes. I should be finished by now, but Matthew said I missed too much last year when we were first getting started here in Far West. So I'm still going."

The Prophet turned and looked toward the south, and then

3

he slowly let his eyes drift toward the west. The temple site had been chosen because it was at the crest of a hill that extended out gradually in all directions. Log houses dotted the hillsides now, but there was still plenty of room. The prairie grass was just turning green for as far as a person could see. In the valleys, where the creeks flowed, the cottonwoods and willows were about to bud out. "It's a beautiful spot, isn't it, Brother Joseph?"

The Prophet slowly turned toward the north, still gazing into the distance. "It surely is. We'll build a good city here—if our enemies will let us."

The boy saw the solemn look return to Joseph Smith's face. "I don't think we have so many enemies here," Joseph said.

"Sometimes, Joseph, we've been our own worst enemy. It's the enemy within I fear as much as any. I don't know how we could have survived the last few years without people like you— you and Matthew and your mother." The Prophet looked directly at Joseph. "I'm truly thankful for you, Joseph."

Joseph was embarrassed, but he managed to say, "We're just glad you're finally with us here in Missouri."

After that, the Prophet walked young Joseph back across the road to Lightner's store, wished him well, and said good-bye.

* * *

At supper that night the family wanted to know what Joseph Smith had talked about. They, like all the Missouri members, had long hoped that the Prophet would come to live in Far West, and now that he had come, somehow it seemed that there was all the more reason to hope for a rich future. Ruth, who was nine now, had met the Prophet only once that she could remember; he had picked her up in his arms and told her how beautiful she was. She had loved him immediately. Little Samuel, who was only four, remembered the Prophet from his visit the previous fall, in 1837. Joseph Smith had tossed him in the air, and then laughed and hugged him.

"Did he say where he is going to live?" Mother asked.

"He didn't mention it, but Bishop Partridge told me he was going to stay at George Harris's house for now. He's going to build a home just across from the temple, by the southwest corner of the square. He'll be only about two blocks from us."

"Did you ask him about Emma?"

"No, I didn't think to."

"You should have, Joseph. You know her health can't be the best, with all they've been through in Kirtland. And her time is not far off."

"Why don't you call on her?" Joseph asked.

"I will some time, but not just yet. Everyone will be hovering about her now. I'll see her on the Sabbath, and then maybe I can call by a little later. I've only met her a time or two; she may not remember me."

Joseph ate his cornbread and salt pork. He was glad that spring had finally come and that the weather was starting to break. He could hardly wait for fresh vegetables.

"But Joseph," Ruth asked, "what else did you talk about? You were gone a long time."

"It took me a while to find him."

"Yes," Mother said, "and Joseph Smith always takes time out to talk to your brother. When Joseph was only nine years old, the Prophet told him that he knew Joseph had a great mission to fulfill."

"I know that," Ruth said. "You've told us a thousand times." She ate quietly for a time and then she said, "I'm nine."

"Yes, and it's about time you began to act like a young lady."

Ruth looked away and didn't say anything. Joseph thought that his mother was sometimes too severe with her.

"But do tell us, Joseph," Sister Williams said, "what else did you talk about?"

Joseph kept eating, but eventually he said, "He told me he thanked the Lord for people like us."

"Did he say that? Were those his words?" Mother reached across the table and put her hand on Joseph's arm. Joseph looked up at her. He could see how much this meant to her.

"Yes, Mother. That's what he said."

Mother looked at Matthew. "We've done our best," she said. Matthew nodded, and Joseph could see that he too was satisfied.

Joseph said, "He's disappointed with some of the Brethren who've turned on us—like the Whitmer brothers. He says it's the enemy within the Church that he fears the most."

"I suppose that's right," Mother said, "but I'm just relieved not to have so many outside, the way we've had in the past."

"Don't be so sure about that," Matthew said softly. It struck Joseph how quiet Matthew had been, as though something were on his mind.

"What do you mean?" Mother asked. Joseph could see the concern in her face. She was still a pretty woman when she smiled, but the last few years had drawn the skin tight around her eyes. She looked harsh when she was worried.

"It's nothing serious," Matthew said.

"But what have you heard?"

Matthew set his fork down, and he leaned forward with his elbows on the table. He was a man now. Eighteen. He looked so much like his father that sometimes it seemed to Joseph that his father had never died. Matthew's dark hair and his solid neck and jaw, just the opposite of Joseph's, gave him a look of strength, even stiffness. "Today—at the gristmill—some of the men didn't know I was a Mormon, and they were talking about us. They said there are too many of us, that we keep coming like flies. One man said he would like to . . . Well, never mind."

"Oh, Matthew, it won't start all over again, will it?"

"What start?" Ruth asked, but no one answered her.

"I don't think so, Mother. There are too many of us this time. I don't think they can drive us out again."

"But will they try?"

"I don't think so. But I'll tell you this much." He looked at Joseph and then back at his mother. "This time, if they do, we'll fight. We'll never let them treat us the way they did in Jackson County."

"Matthew, don't talk that way."

"It's true, Mother," Joseph said. "We'll be ready for them this time."

Matthew's eyes darted at Joseph. "Don't say 'we,' Joseph. I'll be the one to fight for this family."

Joseph was about to disagree, but his mother said, "Oh, please. Let's not talk of such things." Joseph knew she was partly concerned about Ruth and Samuel.

"Mother," Matthew said, "I don't want a fight. But I heard those men today. I heard their vows. I won't run this time. They have no right to take this away from us." He waved his arm to indicate the house. It was a large cabin with carefully hewn logs, chinked inside and out, and with a big rock fireplace. The boys had worked hard to make this new place. And they had built a barn on their land outside town. They had broken the prairie sod in the terrible heat of summer. They had split rails and fenced in fields. And they had already seen their first good crops. Joseph knew that Matthew had meant all of that—the work as well as the results—when he had waved his hand. And Joseph felt the same way. He would not walk away without a fight. In fact, he had been longing for a fight ever since Jackson County. That's what Joseph had not told the Prophet, but it was part of what he meant when he said he didn't feel very religious.

Ruth said, "Mama, I'm afraid they'll hurt Matthew the way they did Father."

No one spoke. Mother didn't answer at first, but after a time she said quietly, "Your father always said that if we fought we would lose. He said we should be Christians and win the love of the old settlers."

Matthew stood up. He pushed his chair back to leave the table. "Yes, and they killed Father," he said.

Chapter 2

On Sunday the Williams family attended church services in the schoolhouse at the town square, not far from the temple site. Joseph Smith gave a long sermon. Joseph Williams was interested as long as the Prophet was talking about Zion and his vision of what Far West would someday be. When the Prophet spoke of the "finer points" of the gospel, however, Joseph's mind tended to wander. At least it was a warm day and the school was not as cold as it had been all winter. But the building was absolutely packed with people, and everyone was forced to squeeze in tight. Joseph held Samuel on his lap.

Most of the Church leaders were there. Bishop Partridge sat next to the Prophet, on the left, and to the right were some of the apostles: Thomas Marsh, David Patten, and Joseph's old friend Parley Pratt. And Brigham Young, who had just arrived in Far West, was up front too. Joseph felt strength from all these men. Somehow it seemed that the enemies of the Church could never prevail again, not with so much solid power in one place. And others were coming. Sidney Rigdon was on his way, and so was Hyrum Smith, the Prophet's brother. Others of the apostles would be moving to Far West when they returned from missions.

The meeting lasted almost three hours and Joseph was greatly relieved when it was over. Everyone lined up and walked past Joseph Smith, thanking him and once again welcoming him to Far West. Some were seeing him for the first time since he had arrived in town, and they greeted him with obvious joy. The Saints had never seemed so confident or full of optimism. And Joseph felt it too. Surely everything would be all right now.

Emma Smith was also being greeted, especially by the sisters. Sister Williams wanted to talk to her, and so the Williamses waited in line for their chance. But Joseph noticed that Matthew stepped aside and said something to the Cox family, who lived a couple of miles west of town and always came in to church on Sundays. For a month now Matthew had been paying special attention to the Coxes, and Joseph knew why. It was Emily, the seventeen-year-old daughter, the one with the dark curly hair and the pretty white teeth. Joseph didn't like her. She had a high-pitched little voice that sounded like sparrow's chatter, and she always let her eyes dart around when she was talking to Matthew. And what was worse, Matthew acted downright stupid when he was around her. He sounded as though he didn't have anything to say but felt he had to keep talking anyway.

Emily had managed to step just a little aside from her parents, and she was saying, "Don't you just love this weather we've been having, Matthew?"

Matthew talked about the good growing season, but he kept stumbling over his words until he sounded like some old settler from Kentucky or Virginia. Joseph moved closer to the Prophet and to Emma. He was glad to get far enough away from Matthew and Emily not to have to listen to them any longer.

Joseph was polite to Emma, and he was happy to shake hands with Joseph Smith again, but then he stepped back and let his mother have her time. Sister Williams was obviously pleased that Emma remembered her, and she accepted Emma's regrets about the death of Brother Williams. Emma was a stately woman, even when so advanced in her pregnancy. She hugged Sister Williams and even Ruth, and she bent down to shake hands with Samuel. But Joseph Smith, like a bear, grabbed Samuel up and embraced him. Samuel laughed and hugged him back. Ruth tried to get by with a handshake, but the Prophet picked her up too. When she landed back on the ground, she straightened her dress and then looked down, avoiding the Prophet's eyes. She looked pretty with her long, light hair and her blue calico dress with the little yellow flowers. The Prophet seemed to sense that he had done the wrong thing, but he laughed, "I'm so sorry, young lady," he said. "I mustn't treat you as a little girl any longer."

"Now she needs to learn to *act* like a young lady," Mother said. Ruth turned red and refused to look at anyone.

Emma reached out and touched the side of Ruth's head. "She's a beautiful girl," she said gently. Ruth glanced up, obviously pleased.

And so, as the family walked home, they all seemed in good spirits, except that Matthew walked a bit ahead and had nothing to say. Finally Sister Williams said, "Matthew, why don't you walk with us?

"I'm just watching for the best path—to keep you out of the mud." He had led them across the street from the square, in front of the store, but Joseph had noticed little mud.

"Well, you could take my arm, you know, and help your poor aged mother."

"You're not aged," Ruth said.

But Joseph said, "Mother, it's not *your* arm he wants to take. He's been looking at some other arms lately.

Matthew turned halfway around, slowing down. He gave

Joseph a less than friendly look and then turned back around and continued on his way. "Joseph," Mother said, "what in the world are you talking about?"

"I'm talking about Emily Cox—that's what." Matthew didn't look back.

"Don't be silly," Mother said. "Matthew is too busy to think of such things yet. And he's too young."

"What do you mean?" Joseph said. "He's eighteen."

"That's all very well, but Matthew is in no position to start thinking about keeping company. That will come in time. And besides, Emily Cox would make a sorry wife for a farmer. She couldn't milk a cow if she had to. She's a pretty girl, but I'm afraid she knows it."

Joseph didn't go inside when they reached home. It was a good day, full of sky and brown earth. Joseph always felt better, less threatened, when the first signs of spring were in the air. He looked out across the valley to the west and tried to picture it the way Joseph Smith had described it. The city would be beautiful, two miles square with broad, straight streets. Around the city would be farms, and the rich land would produce abundance for everyone. No one would be rich, no one poor. It was a nice vision to think about, peaceful and secure. And even though Joseph found little joy in farming, he had a powerful need to feel safe. He had already experienced too much fear and vulnerability.

Except for a light hailstorm that had done a little damage to the young corn, the early growing season had been good, and Matthew was optimistic for their best crop ever. He wanted to buy a larger wagon and a better mule team when the crops came in, and he even talked of buying another parcel of land. What Joseph wanted most was a better horse, but he knew that he was fortunate to have one at all, so he never mentioned it. But Joseph felt good when he heard Matthew talk of the good crops and the prosperity ahead.

One day in June, Joseph saw Porter Rockwell, an old friend from Jackson County, limp across the field and then stop to talk with Matthew. Joseph forgot about it until that afternoon when Matthew said he thought they ought to stop a little early that evening, that he wanted to go to a meeting. Since Joseph was never thrilled about going to meetings, he was only happy that Matthew didn't ask him to go along. But when Matthew got home that night, Joseph noticed that he seemed preoccupied and distant. Mother asked him about the meeting, and he answered vaguely, obviously not eager to tell her about it. She let it go, but the next day, when the boys took a rest from their fence repairing, Joseph brought the subject up.

"What was your meeting about last night, Matthew?"

Matthew had been bent over the little creek getting a drink. As he got up he put his hat back on and said, "Nothing special, Joseph. You know—just a meeting."

"Didn't Brother Rockwell come by and ask you to go?"

"Yes."

"It must have been important then."

"Well, that doesn't really mean much, does it? Lots of times the Brethren encourage us to attend our meetings."

"But this wasn't a regular meeting, was it?"

Matthew lifted off his hat again and wiped his hand across his forehead. "No, it wasn't exactly a regular meeting."

"What was it for then?"

"Listen, Joseph, I can't tell—if I wanted to talk about it, I would. But I don't. Let's just leave it at that."

Matthew turned and started back toward the fence. They were under the cottonwoods that lined the creek. Patterns of sunlight slid across Matthew's old flannel shirt as he walked ahead.

13

"Matthew."

"What?" He kept walking.

"Was it about the rumors we've been hearing? About the old settlers getting heated up again?"

Matthew stopped and turned around. "Joseph, I told you already that I don't want to talk about it."

"That's not fair, Matthew. I have a right to know."

"Why?"

Joseph didn't know why. He couldn't think of anything to say. "Why shouldn't I? I'm old enough."

"Joseph, I was asked not to say anything, all right? I gave my word."

"Can't you even tell me what it was about?

"No."

"People are getting worried, aren't they? I know that."

"Yes, Joseph. There is some reason for concern, but not all that much. We're enlarging the militia—just in case."

"Then that's what your meeting was about. Are you going to be in the militia?"

Matthew said nothing until they reached the fence. But he didn't start work immediately. He put one foot on a rail and looked at Joseph. "Yes, I am going to be in the militia, Joseph. That is one of the things we discussed last night. But I'd appreciate it if you wouldn't say anything to Mother just yet. Maybe nothing will ever come of this. We just need to be ready."

Joseph tried not to show it, but he felt the old fear again— the fear he had known in Jackson County. And he felt angry, too. There was room enough for everyone in northern Missouri. Why couldn't the old settlers just leave the Saints alone?

"Joseph, don't fret about this," Matthew said. "We'll be fine. Now let's get this fence fixed up before the day is gone." They went back to work.

Chapter 3

On the following Sunday the Williamses were in church as usual. Joseph was disappointed when Sidney Rigdon was asked to deliver the sermon. Joseph had heard him speak only a few times, but he knew that Joseph Smith was right, that Brother Rigdon could go on for a long time. But today the man was more fired up than usual. The talk was not so terribly long, but it was full of passion. Joseph couldn't understand exactly what he was trying to say. He talked about salt that had lost its savor, that it should be taken out and trampled under the feet of men. Joseph knew that scripture, but it hardly seemed anything to get so excited about. But Brother Rigdon was usually like that. Joseph really didn't listen all that closely.

Afterward, however, Joseph noticed quite a stir as members gathered in little groups to talk. That in itself was nothing new, but the talk was more excited than usual, more intense, and the children were not allowed to listen.

On the way home Joseph asked Matthew what all the discussion was about. Matthew pretended at first not to know what Joseph meant. But he finally said, "You ought to listen to the sermons more carefully, and then you'd understand."

Joseph decided that Brother Rigdon must have given some new interpretation of doctrine. He really didn't care much about that, so he more or less forgot the matter. But later that week, on Friday, Matthew sent him to the gristmill with a wagon-load of the previous year's corn to grind. When he got there, he put his wagon in line, and then he fed and watered the mules. He would have to wait an hour or two for his turn at the mill.

Three men were leaning against the wagon just ahead of Joseph's, talking and waiting their turns. They were old settlers, not Mormons. Joseph paid little attention to them. He went over to a nearby hickory tree and sat down in the shade, his back against the tree.

Joseph shut his eyes and was almost asleep when he heard the men approach. One said, "Hey, boy, you goin' ta hog up all the shade, or maybe give a parcel of it to some old timers like us?"

Joseph opened his eyes and grinned. "I guess there's enough for all of us," he said.

"Say, you don't sound like no Missouri boy. Where you from?

"I guess I *am* a Missouri boy," Joseph said. "I've lived here seven years."

"Is that so? Whereabouts do you live, son?"

"Far West."

"I see. Yer a Mormon boy." He didn't seem unfriendly. He was a skinny little man with a gray, rather splotchy beard. He walked as though he wanted to limp with both legs.

"Yes, sir. I am."

One of the other men, a larger fellow with stocky arms and legs, said, "I reckon there's better shade some'eres else here-abouts." He and the third man turned and walked toward the mill.

"There's nothing wrong with this shade," Joseph said to the man who had spoken first.

"I s'pose not." But he didn't sit down. "Don't pay too much mind to Garfield there. He come out of Jackson County—was over there when all the troubles come up."

Joseph stood up. He felt self-conscious sitting on the ground when the older man was standing. "Yes, sir. I understand about that. I was there too."

"You was, huh? Well, I guess you seen plenty already for a boy your age."

"Yes, sir. My father was killed."

"In Jackson County?"

"He was beaten there. He died in Clay County later on."

The man shook his head and rubbed his hand along his stubbly beard. His eyes were narrow and yellow, the skin around them creased and folded. "Well, that's a terrible thing," he said. "There was never no call for that. I jist hope it ain't all starting up ag'in."

"Do you think it will?"

"I'm feared it might, son. An' the wors' part is, I think yer people is bringin' it on theirselfs, what with the things they been doin' lately."

"What do you mean?"

"Well, now, I don't want to put no blame on you. Yer jist a boy."

"But I don't even know what you're talking about."

"I guess you know about yer people runnin' the Whitmers off, don't you?"

"No. I don't know about that."

"Well, from what I been hearin', it's so. Garfield over there even says they run out the wives and children while the men was down in Liberty gettin' theirselfs a lawyer. An' not just the

17

Whitmer brothers, neither. It was the Phelps fellow too, and the one named Cowdery."

"I don't think that's right, sir. I haven't heard anything about it. And I don't think our people would do such a thing."

"I hope yer right," the man said. "Because folks 'round here quite liked John Whitmer when he first come up here—and Phelps too. Folks figured there wouldn't be no problem with them. But now when people see them run off like that, they don't take to it."

"Well, sir, people believe too many things they hear. I don't think it was like that. I just think we ought to be able to live together up here in this part of the state. There's plenty of room for all of us."

"I agree to that. As far as I care, there's plenty of space. But some don't see it that way. There's jist so dang many of you that keeps comin'. That's where you make yer mistake, see. I don't understand why you all have to congregate up together in one place. It's that what folks hate. They kin see yer gonna jist take over everything."

"But we just want to be together. We want to build a city—where everyone can be happy. Is that so bad?"

The old man shifted, awkwardly, and then leaned against the tree. It was getting hot now. Joseph could feel the sweat running down his neck. "Well, that's all well and good, I reckon. I shorely admire what yer people kin do. I seen the way they broke the prairie and put up houses. But, see, most folks understood when you come up here that you promised to stay right here in Caldwell County. Where yer makin' yer mistake is sloppin' over into Daviess so much, and now way into Carroll. People don't like that. It looks to them like yer tryin' to take ever'thing fer yerselfs.

Joseph had no reply. He had heard it all before—in Jackson

and again in Clay. But he didn't believe the story about the Whitmers. All the same, to the man he said, "I still think there's room for all of us."

"Well, I guess I do too. You and me's friends, ain't we?" He reached out his hand and Joseph shook it. "I know some folks thinks the Mormons is awful strange and jist don't take to 'em, but me, I figure a man's ways and a man's religion is his own concern. I'm Peter Reed; what's yer name, son?

"Joseph. Joseph Williams." They waited in the shade for some time together, and they talked about the crops and the weather. Joseph liked the man. He thought maybe if Garfield would just come over and chat for a few minutes, he might change his mind about Mormons. Joseph even considered crossing over and striking up a conversation with him. But he had been in situations like that before. They could turn into ugly scenes.

Eventually Joseph got to the front of the line. He hitched up one of his mules to the long drive-pole outside the mill, and then he led the old mule around and around, powering the grindstones. Joseph had plenty of time to think as he walked, and again as he drove the wagon home afterward. When he got home he wanted some answers from Matthew.

But he waited until after supper, when Matthew said he was going to walk back down to the fields for a while. There was a good deal of hoeing that needed to be done, and the light would last awhile yet. So Joseph grabbed a hoe and went with him. Matthew wanted to talk about the crops, as usual, but Joseph asked him, "Matthew, do you know anything about the Whitmers?"

"Yes, I do. They're gone." Joseph could see Matthew's eyes become set. Joseph knew that look. He would not get much out of Matthew tonight.

"But what happened? A man at the mill told me that the sisters and the children got driven out of their houses while the men weren't even home."

"Who told you that?"

"Just an old fellow I talked to over there."

"An old settler?"

"Yes."

"Well, don't believe everything you hear from them." Matthew hoisted his hoe up over his shoulder. "We could sure use some rain in the next few days."

"But do you know anything about it, Matthew? None of our people did a thing like that, did they?"

"Joseph, I don't know exactly what happened—I've heard a few things though. It wasn't as bad as the fellow made it sound. They weren't driven out the way we've been forced out. They were allowed to take all their belongings. No injury was done to them."

"But why? The Whitmers have been with us since the beginning. Remember back in Jackson County when—"

"Joseph, they turned on us! It had to be done. You heard Brother Rigdon's talk."

"What did that have to do with it?"

"Joseph, you never listen in church. Maybe you would understand if you had paid more attention."

"But he was talking about salt losing its savor."

"Yes, Joseph, exactly. And when it does, it's useless and has to be cast out."

"You mean, he meant the Whitmers?"

"Not just them. All the dissenters. The ones who've turned on us and are suing the Prophet, and trying to destroy everything we've worked so hard to build here."

"But Matthew, David and John Whitmer are our friends. Father considered them—"

"Joseph, listen to me. This world is not the way you would like it to be. Not always. I thought you had learned that by now."

"But we should be the ones to do the right things, Matthew. I don't ever want to be on the wrong side—not after what we've been through."

"Joseph, you *are* on the right side. You know that. And if everyone acted the way they ought to, there would be no problem. But people have abused us long enough. We aren't going to let it happen any longer. Sometimes you have to stand up and fight for what's right."

"The man at the mill said we're spreading out too much. He says we promised to stay in this county."

"We promised no such thing, Joseph. They can't make us promise to live in one county. We're free Americans, and we can live where we want to." Matthew put his hoe down, and then he pointed his finger at Joseph's face, the way his father had sometimes done. "Joseph, don't take so much pity on the enemy. If it comes to war, you'll need to know whose side you're on."

"I do know whose side I'm on. And I'll fight too. But I want to fight fair."

"What's fair in a war, Joseph?"

Joseph didn't know. And when he didn't answer, Matthew began to walk. They were beyond the houses that dotted the town lots, not far from their field. Joseph imagined armies marching across the prairies. He had never thought to use the word *war* to describe what they had been through, but maybe that's what it was. He felt a little shiver go through him.

"Listen, Joseph," Matthew finally said, "I hope it doesn't come to that. I don't think it will. And don't worry about the troublemakers. They turned against us, and all we did was tell

21

them to live somewhere else, where they couldn't work against us from within." Joseph didn't reply, but he felt uneasy. He hadn't gotten the answer he wanted. He had wanted Matthew to tell him that the man had lied, that the Whitmers were safe in their homes, where they had always been.

Chapter 4

On the Fourth of July the Saints had a great celebration, the grandest that Joseph had ever seen. It started in the morning, with all the Saints parading to the temple site. The militia led the way, guided by George Hinkle, the chief marshal. The soldiers didn't have much in the way of uniforms, and their weapons were mostly old muskets and homemade swords, but the militia had been drilling all during June and looked fairly respectable. The Church leaders followed close behind: Joseph Smith and his father, the Patriarch; Hyrum Smith; Sidney Rigdon; all the apostles who were in town; Bishop Partridge; and a great many others. All the members followed, and the cavalry brought up the rear. Everyone marched to the patriotic tunes of a rather amateurish band, but what the musicians lacked in skill they made up for in enthusiasm and volume. A huge cloud of dust billowed up behind the parade and floated out across the prairie. Scores of old settlers from outside Far West had come to witness the celebration. Children who had grown up on the prairie had never seen anything like it.

That morning the trunk of a giant white oak tree, sixty feet tall, had been hoisted up as a liberty pole. A carved eagle topped the pole, and a huge American flag fluttered just beneath. It was a wonderful morning, with blue skies and light breezes, and Joseph enjoyed being away from the fields for a day. But he would have given anything to have marched with the militia as Matthew had. Matthew had carried the old musket he had brought from Clay County, and his only uniform was a blue waistcoat that had been Father's. But Joseph thought Matthew looked strong and grown up. Mother said he looked nice, but she was not happy about the weapons. She was especially short with Joseph when he expressed such enthusiasm to join the militia himself.

Joseph marched with the members, holding little Samuel's hand. Samuel had been in good health lately, and he was so excited by the band and the marching that he hopped more than he walked, and he kept laughing for no real reason. Joseph found a stick for him to carry, and Samuel pretended he was a soldier, like Matthew. He tried to look stern, but he broke into giggles when Joseph looked at him.

Joseph saw many of the Saints he hadn't seen in some time—people who had been with them in the early years in Missouri, but who were now spread out in the smaller settlements in Caldwell County or in the town in Daviess County that Joseph Smith had named Adam-ondi-Ahman. Newel Knight was there, with his new wife, Lydia, and their baby boy. Joseph was reminded of Brother Knight's first wife, Sally, who had suffered so much before she had died in Clay County.

Following the parade was the laying of the cornerstones of the temple. The women all stood in front with the younger children, surrounding the excavation, and the men stood behind. Various Church leaders were called out to set the stones in place with heavy oak levers, each time with the assistance of twelve strong men. Joseph Smith had a way of lending dignity and importance to such occasions, and he was in fine form today. He was wearing a sky-blue coat and white pantaloons, with a sword strapped to his side. His introductions and comments were all done rather formally, but with his usual brightness and good nature.

All this was followed by an oration. Joseph knew that Sidney Rigdon, as usual, was to be the orator. Joseph moved out of the circle and sat down on the grass beyond, as many of the younger people did. Ruth found Joseph and sat down on the grass beside him. Sidney Rigdon stood on a platform that had been constructed for the day's events. Behind him sat some of the Church leaders and several non-Mormon dignitaries from surrounding counties. Brother Rigdon projected his voice out over the crowd in his usual grand style. It was the sort of talk a person would expect at a Fourth of July celebration, full of patriotism and fancy words. Joseph watched the flag and the sky and hoped that the talk would not be terribly long and tedious. As it turned out, it was plenty long enough, but it gradually began to catch Joseph's attention. Brother Rigdon became increasingly adamant and loud as he proclaimed the glories of America, but toward the end he didn't hide his anger about the treatment the Saints had received in a land that was supposed to be free. Joseph began to feel uncomfortable. Many of the old settlers were still there, and Joseph wondered what they would think.

"We have not only, when smitten on one cheek, turned the other," Brother Rigdon shouted, "but we have done it again and again, until we are wearied of being smitten, and tired of being trampled on." Joseph watched the men on the platform, the old settlers, but they seemed not to be disturbed. And actually, why should they? Joseph told himself that what Brother Rigdon was saying was true—and should be said. "That mob that comes on us to disturb us, it shall be between us and them a war of extermination; for we will follow them till the last drop of their blood is spilled, or else they will have to exterminate us; for we will carry the seat of war to their own houses and their own families, and one party or the other shall be utterly destroyed."

Joseph felt a chill. He was both thrilled and frightened. It felt good to hear him say such things, and to say them with the old settlers listening. This would let them know that the Saints would take no more at their hands. And yet . . . the words were so strong: blood spilling. War. Extermination.

But Brother Rigdon was not finished. "We will never be the aggressors; we will infringe on the rights of no people, but shall stand for our own until death." His voice reached an intense pitch as he shouted the last words. "We this day then proclaim ourselves free, with a purpose and a determination that never can be broken—no, never! No, never! NO, NEVER!"

Suddenly all the Church members were waving their hats in the air and shouting. They cried "Hosanna" several times, each time louder than the time before. Joseph had not shouted, but he had felt the excitement, the pleasure. It was a declaration, an announcement to the world, that the Saints were a power to be respected. But Joseph watched a young man, a Missourian, who was leaning against his wagon and standing back from the crowd a little way. He seemed confused. He turned to his wife and said something, and then the two of them got in the wagon. He flipped the reins, and his team pulled the wagon onto the road. As the wagon rolled away Joseph watched the man as he twisted his head around to watch the crowd. Joseph wondered what he would say to his neighbors when he got home.

Joseph looked up at the flag on the liberty pole. It seemed to represent the strength the Mormons now possessed. "Hosanna," Joseph said, only to himself.

"What did you say?" It was Ruth. She and Joseph were both standing up now, and she was still next to him.

Joseph looked at her for a moment. "I said 'hosanna,' same as the rest."

Ruth looked concerned. She was looking up at Joseph, with her eyes squinted against the sun. Everyone said she looked like Joseph, and Joseph could see himself reflected in her face now. At the same age he had been forced to understand the hatred of the old Missouri settlers—but Ruth had seen even more. She was a serious girl with a strong sense of foreboding, and a clear understanding of the power of violence. "What did he mean, Joseph? Would we really spill people's blood?"

"It was just a warning. That's all."

"Joseph, I remember before," Ruth said, "when they would scream and shoot their guns, and set houses on fire. I was little, but I remember."

Joseph remembered too. "We won't let it happen again," he said, but he felt the old fear rise to his throat.

* * *

Joseph and his family went home. They took the rest of the day off for a holiday, except that Matthew did some repair work on the harnesses. The next day was hot and humid, and the morning after that thunderstorms were crashing across the plains. In the afternoon the rain fell hard for a while and the lightning flashed incessantly. The boys came in from their work and waited out the storm. Afterward, they went back to the field and were relieved to see that the corn was not damaged. But little work could be done in the mud.

As they walked back to town, Joseph noticed something missing. He couldn't think what it was for a moment, and then he realized that the liberty pole was gone. He told Matthew, and the two of them walked past their house to the town square. Many of the Saints had gathered there and were standing in little groups. The liberty pole was splintered halfway up, the top half angling downward, the flag lying in the mud.

"Lightning," Matthew said.

Joseph didn't speak. For some reason he felt uneasy.

Chapter 5

In spite of Sidney Rigdon's speech, July was calm. Rumors and threats went about, and the people in Carroll County were openly hostile to the Saints in DeWitt, but nothing serious happened, and the Saints began to feel confident that the old settlers were not about to try anything. Not only that, the Mormon militia had grown a great deal, and many more weapons had been procured. Hundreds of Saints were moving in, many of them settling around Far West, but even more in Adam-ondi-Ahman, or "Diahman," as the town was coming to be known. These added numbers gave the Saints more reason for confidence, but it gave the Missourians more reason for complaint.

Matthew drilled with the militia and attended weekly meetings. But Joseph noticed that Matthew talked less about the farm and the future, and he became cranky with Joseph over little things. It was not any easy time for Joseph. He had so little to look forward to. He hardly ever saw any boys his own age because he was always working, and when Matthew wasn't optimistic, wasn't pumping enthusiasm into him, the work seemed endless and rather pointless.

One day early in August, Brother Hinkle knocked on the

door early in the morning, before Ruth and Samuel were out of bed. Matthew went to the door, and then stepped outside. In a few minutes he came back in. "Joseph," he said, "some of us in the militia have been asked to ride with Joseph Smith and some of the other brethren to Daviess County. You'll need to look after things for a few days. Be sure to feed the animals and—"

"What is it, Matthew?" Mother asked. She had been sitting in front of a tiny mirror on the wall, tying up her hair. She turned now as she tied her little white cap on.

"I don't know the whole story, Mother. There were some troubles at an election in Gallatin yesterday."

"What kind of troubles?

"I guess some of the men in Gallatin tried to keep our brethren from Diahman from voting. There was a fight."

Joseph had been pulling on his boots, but he stood up now. "How bad of a fight?" he asked.

"I can't tell you any more than that," Matthew said. "That's all I know." But he was avoiding Joseph's eyes, and Joseph knew there was more to the story.

"Was anyone hurt?" Mother asked.

"No one knows, Mother. Some people are saying that a couple of our men were killed, but that may not be right. We're going up just to check on the situation. Joseph Smith wants to settle things before they get serious."

"Serious?" Mother said. "Serious, Matthew? What are you telling me? That some of our people are dead and it's not serious?" She stood up. Joseph could see the familiar fear—the panic—in her eyes. She had said so many times that she couldn't live through another experience like the one in Jackson County.

"But, Mother, it wasn't a planned attack. Maybe we can settle things down before they get worse."

"Matthew, are you riding right into Gallatin—where the troubles are?"

"Well, yes."

Tears spilled from Sister Williams's eyes. She sat down. Matthew walked to her and put his arm around her shoulders.

"Now listen, Mother. We're not going for a fight. We're going to settle matters. I'll be back before you know it. Joseph will look after things here."

"Matthew," Joseph said, "if they attack here while you're gone, I don't have a weapon. I need a gun of some kind."

"Joseph!" his mother hissed. "You will *not* have a gun. You are a boy, and no one will kill a boy. As soon as you take up a rifle, you're a soldier, and they'll shoot you down the same as anyone else."

"I'm *not* a boy, Mother. You have to—"

"That's enough, Joseph," Matthew said firmly. "Now listen, both of you. There is no war. No one is going to attack Far West. It would take a whole army to do that. But Mother is right, Joseph. You're too young to carry a weapon. I'll be back in two or three days, and everything will be fine."

"Where are you going, Matthew?" It was Ruth. She was peering down from the opening in the loft, her pretty hair falling down around her face.

"You jump back in bed a bit longer," Mother said. "I haven't fixed breakfast yet."

"Where's Matthew going?" Ruth looked worried. She was only half awake, and she acted confused, as though she had just awakened from a bad dream.

"Ruth," Matthew said, "I'm going with Joseph Smith for a couple of days. It's nothing to worry about."

"Why did Joseph say he needed a gun?"

Matthew stared up at Ruth for a time without answering.

Joseph looked away, down at the floor. "You know Joseph," Matthew said. "He's wanted a gun for a long time."

"But he said someone might attack us."

"No, Ruth, no one's attacking us."

"Get back in bed," Mother said.

Ruth was looking at her mother as though she hadn't heard. Joseph looked up at her, and their eyes met for a moment. "I'm scared," Ruth said. "They won't make us leave our house again, will they?"

"No, Ruth," Matthew said. "Don't worry about that."

But Ruth was looking at Joseph, not at Matthew. She wanted Joseph to answer. But he said nothing. He looked away.

* * *

Matthew left that morning, and Joseph put in a hard day's work. All day he tried to think what Matthew would have done, and then he did the same. But his mind was not on his work, and the day dragged by slowly. After supper he walked over to Bishop Partridge's house to see what news might have come from Gallatin. The bishop was not home, but Sister Partridge had good news. The brethren had gotten word that the first report was wrong. No one had been killed at the election—the Saints were all right. "I think your brother will be back in a day or two," she said. "Joseph Smith plans to stay on just long enough to make things right with the old settlers in Gallatin." She had a mild manner, much like her husband's, and a gentle voice. Joseph suddenly felt much better. He thanked her and hurried home.

Mother relaxed a good deal when Joseph brought the news. Joseph watched the muscles around her mouth and eyes loosen, and he felt the life come back into her movements. But she only said, "I'll feel better when he's home with us." Joseph felt the same way, and yet it bothered him a little to know how much his mother needed Matthew's strength, and how little he could give her himself.

Matthew did not get back until almost midnight on Thursday. The next morning he seemed less than anxious to talk about his experience. He said the brethren who had tried to vote had been only a handful, John Lee and some of the others from Daviess County. They had taken on a whole mob and had done all right for themselves. Samuel Butler had found himself a good oak stick and had cracked a dozen or so heads before he was finished. Joseph couldn't help smiling about that.

"Did they vote?" Joseph wanted to know.

"I guess some of them did."

"It sounds like those people up in Daviess might think twice before they try to take on the Mormons again," Joseph said, and now he was grinning.

But Matthew didn't smile. "I guess maybe they will," he said. "But we're outnumbered there. We need to send a great many more of the new Saints up to settle around Diahman."

Joseph tried to find out what else Matthew had been doing, but Matthew answered briefly, even sounded a little annoyed. Joseph decided that Matthew didn't want to talk very much in front of Ruth, and so he let the subject go. But gradually he could see there was something bothering Matthew. Samuel was overjoyed to have Matthew home, but Matthew had little patience with his chatter. Samuel loved to sit on Matthew's lap and nestle close against his chest, but this morning Matthew set Samuel down after only a minute or two.

After the little ones had gone to bed that night, Joseph tried to get Matthew to talk. "It must be nice," Joseph said, "to ride with Brother Joseph and the other men. Did ol' Jonathon keep up with the other horses all right?"

"He did well enough." Matthew glanced at his mother.

"Tell me more about Brother Butler. How many do you think he knocked down?"

"I don't know, Joseph. Someone said ten or a dozen."

Joseph laughed. "Did he crack their skulls?"

"I don't know, Joseph. I hope not." Matthew walked to the window, the one with the glass in it—glass Matthew had ordered from St. Louis. The other windows were still covered with thin sheets of oiled paper, but Matthew said at the end of the season he would get more glass. The light was fading now, but no one had lit the lamp. Matthew was turning into a silhouette against the window.

"I think that's enough of that kind of talk, Joseph," Mother said. She had just given up her mending and was sitting quietly in her chair by the fireplace, even though there was no fire now. Joseph felt the darkness in the room, felt the gloom in his brother.

"Matthew," Joseph said, "aren't some of the men in the militia just seventeen?"

Matthew didn't answer. He continued to look out the window into the grayness. "Joseph," Mother said, "we've heard all we're going to hear about you and the militia."

"You can say that now, Mother, and maybe Joseph Smith would say the same. But next year I'll be seventeen, and then I can join."

"Listen, Joseph," Matthew said. "In the first place, it is not so exciting as you think it is. And in the second place, one from a family is enough."

"I know lots of families who have more than one in the militia," Joseph said.

"I didn't say there weren't. But one is still enough, especially if one of them is the head of the family."

"Well, then, maybe next spring you should get out of the

militia, and I'll get in. Then if anything happens, it won't hurt the family so much."

"All right. That's enough," Mother said. "Listen to the two of you fighting for the right to die. What is it about men—and *boys*—that makes them love the sight of blood?" Matthew turned around and looked at her, but she didn't look up. She was staring down at her hands in her lap. The features of her face were lost in the darkness now, but Joseph could feel the rigidity of her muscles, her anger. "Your father would be disappointed in you," she said less stridently. "You know how he hated all these contentions."

"I don't want this either, Mother," Matthew said. "I want to live in peace. And I want to go on a mission as soon as I can get things ready here. But Mother, there will be no missions if we don't stop these people. They hate us—more than you can even imagine."

"What do you mean, more than I can imagine? I don't have to imagine, Matthew. Neither do you. We've seen it all before. I simply can't stand it if it comes again."

"We'll be all right this time, Mother," Matthew said.

Mother's face lifted toward Joseph. "Joseph, I want you to give me a promise," she said. "I want you to promise that you'll stay with me. If troubles come again, I don't want to be alone."

"But Mother, I might *have* to help. I might be called out. The old settlers wouldn't do anything to women and little children. You said that yourself."

"Joseph, I don't want to be alone."

"Well, I don't see what difference it makes. If I can't have a gun, what could I do for you anyway?"

"Joseph, promise me."

Joseph didn't answer. Matthew stepped toward him. "Joseph, Mother needs someone. Promise her."

Joseph continued to sit and stare at the darkened table in front of him. "I'm sorry," he finally said, "but I can't make that promise."

Chapter 6

Joseph was not forced into a promise. Matthew apparently knew better than to push too hard—he had learned that lesson with Joseph before. But Mother had little to say to Joseph. This bothered him, but he had other things to consider. A mother always wanted a boy to stay a boy, but it couldn't always be that way. Besides, Matthew claimed that being in the militia was nothing great, but Joseph noticed that he talked rather differently that Sunday when Emily Cox wanted to know about Matthew's excursion to Daviess County.

"We were lucky this time," he said. "We didn't have to fire a single weapon. But we were ready if it had come to that."

"Matthew, weren't you scared?" Emily asked.

"I guess anyone feels some fear at a time like that," he said, nodding seriously.

"I'm sure I'd turn and run off," she said, and she smiled and showed her dimples. "I'm not brave like you, Matthew."

"Well, I don't claim to be brave. But a man has to do his part, you know."

"And I guess it helps to be so strong," she said, and she touched Matthew's shoulder.

Joseph watched Matthew's color rise, and that was not something that happened to Matthew very often. Joseph was embarrassed for him. It wasn't even Matthew talking. Joseph was standing with Ruth some distance away, and they were both pretending not to listen, looking off in other directions most of the time, but when Emily touched Matthew's shoulder, both Joseph and Ruth took a good look and then glanced at each other.

"I guess I'm not weak," Matthew finally said.

Joseph looked back to see Emily flashing that pretty smile again, obviously enjoying Matthew's discomfort. And the rest of the day Joseph kept seeing that smile and those dark eyes. Joseph thought he had never seen a girl so pretty—or so stupid. But why did he find himself wishing all the more that he were in the militia? He even wished that he had shoulders like Matthew's.

Joseph found such emotions confusing and uncomfortable, but what was worse was being around Matthew these days. The boys put in hard days together, working in the garden and keeping the weeds down in the cornfields, but Matthew had little to say. At first Joseph thought it was because he had refused to make the promise to Mother, but when he brought the subject up, Matthew passed it off with less concern than Joseph expected. Matthew continued to go to his meetings. As far as Joseph could tell, they were militia meetings, but Matthew would not say a word about them. In fact, always the day after, Matthew was especially unwilling to talk. Joseph tried a dozen ways to get Matthew to reveal what was going on, but he was impenetrable.

It wasn't until early in September that Joseph first found out that Joseph Smith was going to be tried in Daviess County. He had been accused of forcing Judge Adam Black to sign some sort of papers. Joseph didn't really understand what it was all about, and he couldn't get much out of Matthew. But Matthew had been there. The incident had occurred when Matthew had gone with the brethren to Gallatin. Matthew, however, would only say, "We went to the judge's place and asked him to sign a statement that he would do all he could to keep the peace. I guess afterward he said we threatened his life and made him sign."

"Did anyone threaten him?" Joseph asked.

"No, of course not. But a couple of the men did get a little carried away. They said more than they needed to—or at least it seemed so to me."

But that was the only reservation Matthew would express, even though Joseph tried to push him to say more. "Matthew, why won't you talk about it?" Joseph finally asked. "What's the matter with you lately? You act like you have to keep everything a secret from me."

"I tell you what I think you need to know," Matthew said, and that was all. He went back to work. But he was not intent upon the work, not the way he had always been before. All the rumors about troubles in Daviess County, and now in Carroll County, didn't bother Joseph so much as the feeling that something was wrong with Matthew.

* * *

Joseph tried to find out as much as he could each day. He would ask anyone he saw what was happening in the surrounding counties. There were so many rumors it was difficult to determine what was actually going on. Joseph Smith stood trial, along with Lyman Wight, but nothing was really settled. For a time an open battle in Daviess County seemed certain, with the Missourians and the Mormons each gathering into camps for protection. Militias from several counties hurried to the aid of the old settlers, and generals Doniphan and Atchison were sent in by the governor to attempt to restore the peace. The generals,

38

old friends of the Mormons from Clay County, seemed to feel that the Saints were being falsely accused of aggression, and they did their best to settle the problems.

Gradually things quieted somewhat in Daviess, but they only got worse in Carroll County. In the little town of DeWitt, near where the Grand River emptied into the Missouri, a little colony of Mormons had been growing too fast for the liking of the old settlers. Hostilities got worse, until by early October the town was under siege, and the Mormons were cut off and being starved out. Joseph Smith and Lyman Wight had taken a small force and had managed to get into town. They hoped to bolster the Saints and help them defend themselves until an agreement could be reached or the governor perhaps would send help.

Everyone wondered what was happening and what would follow in Far West if open fighting broke out. But the reports from DeWitt were sketchy and contradictory. The leaders in Far West hardly knew what to expect.

All the same, Matthew and Joseph went to the fields each day, as most of the Mormons did. The harvest was on now, and the crops had been good. Maybe things would quiet down if the matter could be settled in DeWitt as it apparently had been in Daviess. There was even talk of the Mormons buying out all the old Missourians in Daviess County. Maybe someday the Saints would possess all of upper Missouri, and the tensions would be gone forever. Everyone believed that somehow the Lord would make a way that Jackson County would once again be the center of Zion. It just didn't seem possible that the Saints would ever lose their last hold on Missouri, their land of promise.

On Wednesday morning, the tenth of October, Bishop Partridge came to the field where Joseph and Matthew were working. Joseph saw him coming between the rows of corn and waved to him. "May I talk to you boys?" he said as he approached.

He looked worried and he didn't look well to Joseph. He never had completely recovered from the beating he had taken when he was tarred and feathered in Independence. Joseph thought he had begun to gain back some of his vigor in Far West, but now he looked solemn standing there in the field in his dark suit of clothes.

"How are you, Bishop?" Joseph asked.

"Fine, Joseph. But I have a favor to ask of you—if it's all right with Matthew."

"Sure," Joseph said.

"You'd better listen to what it is first—before you answer. It involves some danger."

"Oh, don't worry about that," Joseph said, hopeful that Matthew wouldn't put a stop to whatever it was Bishop Partridge wanted him to do.

"We haven't heard a word from DeWitt for two days," the bishop said. "We need to get someone in there. I thought of you, Joseph. You're a good rider, and you've been here in Missouri long enough to talk like a Missourian if you have to. Both Hyrum and Father Smith agree with me that you'd be the best choice. They wanted me to ask you to go."

"Yes, Bishop, I can do it. I know the talk. And I know my way."

"Listen, Bishop," Matthew said, "I think I'd better go. I can do the same."

"I know, Matthew. I thought of that, but you're in the militia. You've been seen before. The Carroll County militia was in Daviess when you were there with Joseph Smith. I'm afraid if they caught you, they might be awfully rough with you."

"But I hate to see Joseph go. He's only—"

"I know how you feel, Matthew. I hate to see anyone go. But I think—and the Brethren agree—that Joseph has a good chance of making it. He has a good head for such things, and he knows his way about. If he's caught, they may just send him home. He's tall, but he has a boy's face, and no one would take him for a soldier."

Joseph hardly liked that last, but he was still eager to go. "I'm sure I can do it," he said.

"The thing is, Bishop," Matthew said, "Mother is awfully concerned, what with me in the militia and all. She's scared that she could be left alone out here."

Bishop Partridge looked down at the earth. He was almost as tall as the corn that stood in rows on each side of him. Finally he looked up, his face solemn. "I understand that, Matthew, but he seems the best boy to do it. We simply must get word. They could be massacred by now, for all we know."

"All right," Matthew said, nodding firmly. "I'll talk to Mother. Joseph, don't go home first. Bishop, won't he need to do something to look more like a Missouri boy?"

Bishop Partridge looked at Joseph, and slowly a quiet smile spread across the bishop's face. "I think not," he said. There was Joseph with his old floppy felt hat, his worn-out boots, and his trousers covered with dirt. Pieces of corn husk stuck here and there to his old homespun shirt, and under his hat his face was burned a deep brown. "No, I think not."

"I reckon I ain't much to look at, feller, but I kin shore ride," Joseph said, grinning.

"You'll pass," Matthew said, and he even smiled.

"And listen, Joseph," the bishop said, "do what you have to do. I don't even know how to tell you to get past the guards and into DeWitt, but find a way."

"I'll find a way, don't worry, Bishop," Joseph said excitedly.

"All right, get your horse and go to Hyrum Smith's place. He wants to talk to you before you leave. You'll need a coat and some blankets; you could end up out in the cold tonight."

"I'll get those for you, Joseph," Matthew said. "I'll meet you at Brother Smith's."

Joseph started to run toward the barn to get his horse, but he heard Bishop Partridge say, "God bless you, Joseph."

Chapter 7

Joseph pushed his old horse as hard as he dared. It was almost forty miles to DeWitt and he hadn't gotten away until after nine o'clock. He also did a lot of thinking along the way. He decided to ride directly for DeWitt and see whether he could bluff his way past the guards. It would be well after dark—maybe he could sneak into the settlement somehow. But he had to make it. This was his first chance to prove himself, to do something important, and he was not going to fail.

He had brought some food, but he ate little of it until late in the day when he simply had to stop to let his horse rest and graze for a time. When he finally pushed on and neared DeWitt, it was getting quite late. Joseph guessed it was close to eleven o'clock. But he stayed on the road that led into town, feeling he needed that guidance until he was close to the settlement. Eventually he saw a fire ahead and assumed that it must be an outpost set up by the old settlers who had surrounded the Mormon settlement. But at least this was a chance to see just how difficult it was going to be to get past them and into town.

He tried to ride on by, but a man by the fire stood up and stepped in front of him. "Where you goin' to, boy?" he said.

Then another man—actually a boy about Joseph's age—stepped out of the dark and stood next to the first man. The one in front of Joseph was good-sized, wearing a striped blanket coat and a coonskin hat. He was the one who did the talking.

"DuWitt," Joseph said.

"What for?"

"What difference do it make? Cain't a man go to a place if he wants to?"

"No, a man cain't—not always—nor kin a young calf like you neither. 'Specially in the dark."

"Why not? Ain't no one ever stopped me from coming here afore."

"What is it you want here, boy?"

Joseph had hoped a few sentences might reassure them, and that he would be allowed to pass. "I'm comin' to help my uncle what lives over in these parts. He fell an' broke his shoulder, an' he needs some help gittin' his corn in. My pa sent me over."

"Who's yer uncle?"

"Azael Crawford. You know 'im?" Joseph leaned back on his saddle, as though he needed to stretch his back. He wanted to seem natural, if he could.

"No, I don't. An' I guess I know jist about ever'body over in these parts."

"Uncle Azael is outside of town a little way, over right along the Grand."

"Then how come you said you was going to DuWitt?" Joseph saw the boy grin as he looked around the shoulder of the bigger man. Some of his bottom teeth were missing. The fire-light made the two faces orange on one side, black on the other.

"I jist meant I gotta go *through* DuWitt, thass all."

"You better git yer story straight, boy. It don't sound quite right to me. How come yer ridin' this late at night?"

"Pa made me finish up helpin' him at home afore he let me go. I tol' 'im I wanted to git goin' earlier. I prob'ly won't git two hours sleep afore I'm back out workin'."

"I'm sorry, boy, but that don't sound like no likely story to me. Ain't nobody makes a ride like that at night. I think you been sent to take letters to Joe Smith. Now you tell the truth. Yer a Mormon boy, ain't yuh?"

"He don't sound zackly right to me," the boy said. "He don't talk zackly right."

"Don't call me no dang Mormon," Joseph said. "We drove the Mormons out of Clay County—an' we don't want no more of 'em neither."

"You say yer from Clay?"

"Thass right."

"Where 'bouts?"

"South o' Liberty. Along the river, in by the bluffs."

"How long you been in Clay?"

"Four year, I think it is. We come out here from Ohio."

"Maybe thass why he talks like 'at," the boy said.

"Maybe. An' maybe not. You carryin' letters, boy? Like maybe one to Joe Smith?"

"I know who Joe Smith is. I wouldn't carry no letter to his grave. An' I don' 'preciate you talkin' that way."

"Wull, thass jist fine, but I ain't takin' no chances. You kin go out around DuWitt an' still git where yer goin.'"

Joseph knew the man couldn't be pushed, but he thought it would be more natural to persist just a little. "'Cept I only know one way—thass the way I allus went, right on through DuWitt. I'll shore git lost, off the road in the night."

"Thass the mistake you made in comin' after dark. You kin sit right here by this fire if you want—all night long—but you

45

ain't goin' fu'ther on down the road, not so long as I'm keepin' watch."

"Least tell me what's the best way to go then, if I cain't use the road. I don't see what difference it—"

"Head off thataway, hold straight for over a mile, and then foller the Grand down to where you say he lives. But I don't think there's no Crawford down there. I know I never heard of him."

"He jist moved down here lass year," Joseph said.

"Thass what you say. An' maybe you know somethin' about Clay County, but lots of Mormons was there, an' you jist might be one of 'em."

"It don't do no good to talk to you," Joseph said. "I kin see that."

Joseph turned his horse toward the west, the direction the man had pointed. "An' don't try to come 'round back to the road," the man yelled after him. "We got guards all up an' down it. An' close in we got everythin' good and blocked off. Ain't no one gittin' into 'em. You kin go back an' tell yer people that."

Joseph kept riding, but he heard it all. He had thought of doing just what the man had warned him of. He would have to think of something else now. He kept going until he was well out of sight, and then he stopped. He got down and let his horse rest while he thought.

There was only one way into the settlement, and Joseph knew what it was: the Missouri River. He decided to loop back around the outpost, and then head south to the river. If he could find some sort of raft or boat maybe he could float down to DeWitt.

There was no moon, and a cloud cover was moving in. When Joseph reached the wood, near the river, the brush was so thick that he had to get off and lead his horse. But he eventually broke through to the riverbank. At first he thought of walking down the shore to the settlement, but he knew there would be guards when he got closer. He had to get rid of his horse, and he had no choice but to leave her in the woods, tied up. He hoped he would get back to her the next day.

Joseph headed upstream, watching for anything he could use to get down the river. But he walked over a mile and could hardly see anything. The night had become bitterly cold, and a chilling wind was blowing down the river valley. He suspected a storm was blowing in.

He didn't have much time—the river would be no help to him in the daytime, when he could be spotted. When he came upon a ferry landing, he almost went on by, but then he realized that there would probably be a small boat on the ferry. Joseph stood for a minute or two and watched the run-down old raft that was rocking and creaking against a little dock. He had never stolen anything. He wondered what he should do now. The bishop had said to do anything to get into DeWitt, that lives were at stake. And Hyrum Smith had said the same thing.

Joseph knew that a ferryman had to live close by, probably in an old shack just above the riverbank, if he fit the usual pattern. But it was too dark to see far enough to know for sure. He walked quietly out on the dock, and then he stepped down onto the ferry. He felt his way toward the front, beyond the little cabin. The boat was just in front of the cabin, exactly where Joseph had thought it would be. But the problem was to get the boat off the ferry and hang on to it in the current long enough to get aboard. He found an oar behind the boat, and he decided he could push the boat part way off, get in, and then push himself off with the oar.

He soon found, however, that the boat was quite heavy, and it groaned as he pulled it across the timbers of the ferry. But he was gradually getting it to the edge. He moved around behind it and shoved. But the boat caught on a plank and rolled onto its side, knocking against the deck. A dog barked, and then after a few seconds it barked again. Joseph held still for some time, but when he heard nothing more, he moved around to the front of the boat and pulled it toward the ridge that lined the edge. He was almost ready to slide it over the top and into the water when the dog began to bark again, and a light appeared above the river bank.

Joseph lifted and pulled and then shoved hard, and the boat was halfway over the ridge. Now he could hear the dog coming down the hill, no longer barking, but grunting and running hard. Joseph shoved again and then jumped. But he was only half in the boat, and his legs were in the water. The boat twisted and then began to pick up speed. It was leaning under Joseph's weight, and he feared it would swamp at any moment. He heard a man yell in the distance, and then a bullet whizzed through the air. Joseph clung to the boat.

He was soon out of range of the man with the gun, but he was still half in the water. He waited until the boat rocked downward a little, and then he reached and caught the other side. The boat dipped and picked up water, but Joseph pulled himself across quickly and rolled inside. He was safe—for the moment. But after a few seconds he realized how terribly cold he was. He sat up and felt around for the oar. He needed to stay far enough out in the channel not to be noticed as he approached town, yet he also needed to be able to move toward the settlement quickly at just the right moment. But the oar was gone. It had apparently tipped out when the boat had rolled on the ferry. He was moving fast now, and he had no control at all. Joseph knew he was in trouble, but he couldn't think what to do.

For a moment he gave way to despair. He hated this river

that had always gotten in his way. He sat and watched the dim shadows go by. He could see very little. He felt helpless and pitifully weak.

Joseph's legs were freezing; his whole body was beginning to shake. He couldn't even tell how far from the shore he was. He knew he had to get closer in, somehow, to have any chance of getting to the settlement. There was nothing in the boat, however, nothing at all. But then Joseph thought of his boots. He pulled one off and held it over the side and let it scoop up water until the boat began to pull to the left. The current was very strong, but the boat was pulling toward the shore, if only gradually. Maybe it wasn't enough. He had no idea how far he had come. His hands were freezing, but he kept the boot down in the water as long as he could stand it, until he felt the boat moving into slower water, nearer to the shore. He couldn't get in too close, not yet, or he might be spotted by guards along the riverbank, but he had to be close enough to make his move when the time came.

He saw a fire on the bank ahead. He didn't know whether it would be the old settlers' camp, or the settlement where the Mormons were. But he knew he had to get closer to have a chance of seeing what was there. He dug the boot all the way under the water. He felt the boat edge toward the shore. His arms ached from the strain and the cold. The fire came up fast. Joseph could see one man sitting by it; he decided it must be a guard for the old settlers. He lifted the boot up and let the boat glide by silently.

But then he realized that the shore was moving away, that the river was beginning to widen. He was back into the faster current. He must be nearing the mouth of the Grand River. He plunged the boot back into the water, but too suddenly, and it pulled from his hands and was gone. He quickly got his other boot off, gripped it as tightly as he could, and then dug it into the water.

Then there were more fires. It might not be the Saints, but he had to gamble that it was. The boat was pulling around, but it was still well out into the stream, and the fires were coming up all too fast. Once he got past the mouth of the Grand, he would never make it back. If he got to shore and was not in the right settlement, he was in trouble. But Joseph knew that a large group of Mormons from Canada had recently arrived. They wouldn't have log houses yet, but would be camping out. He had to assume that the fires were theirs.

Joseph held the boot in the water as long as he could, but he could see that he was going to go on by, that he simply could not get the boat to shore. He waited until the last possible second, and then he let the boot go, jumped up and threw his coat off, and dived into the water. Joseph was not a great swimmer, and he was terrified. He didn't feel the cold, didn't even think about it. He drove his arms at the water, struggling to get to the fires. But the current was still carrying him downstream and it was difficult to keep himself pointed toward the shore. He flailed and kicked and fought the water, exactly as he knew he shouldn't, but he was beginning to realize that he was in real danger.

He could see the fires, and they were not getting any closer. He kept struggling and kicking, fighting to keep his head up at times, but he was still moving with the current more than through it. Seconds went by that seemed like minutes. He didn't know that he was beginning to tire; he just felt that he was getting nowhere and that he was in terrible trouble. He felt anger beneath everything else. He hated to fail. There was nothing he hated more.

Then, almost suddenly, he was out of the swift current and into the more placid water closer to the shore. But he was tired.

He could feel it now. His arms didn't want to keep pumping, and his legs were heavy, but he wanted to live. He wanted to make it to the bank. His body, however, couldn't seem to work hard enough. He fought the impulse to give up, and concentrated on swimming more efficiently, getting the most out of each stroke. But it was useless. His arms wouldn't push anymore. He was going down. "Help me, Lord," he said. He wanted to cry out. He wanted to find some extra strength, but he was sinking below the water, and he could do nothing.

"Help me," he said again in his mind, and he tried to fight one more time, but his arms only flopped weakly in front of him, and then his head went under. All was silent and black for a moment. Then his feet touched the bottom. He pushed upward with all his strength, and his head popped above the water again. The water was not very deep. He just needed to get a little closer to shore. He struggled with his arms again, and went down once more. But this time his head was still out of the water as his feet touched. The current took him off his feet immediately, but he fought forward, and this time when he went down, the water was only to his shoulders. He tried to walk now, tried to push his way with his legs, but the mud clung to his feet and made the going almost impossible.

But he could stand, and for a few seconds he merely waited for breath and for what power he could still muster. He would not die. Not in this river. He pushed forward again, and then the bank began to ascend rather abruptly. He hadn't realized how close he had been. He gave one last effort and clambered up the incline out of the water, but then he collapsed, his legs still in the river and his face in the mud of the bank.

Joseph couldn't think. He couldn't move. His mind whirred for some time, and he felt warm, then hot. A strange dream flowed in and out of his consciousness. He was riding his horse, and it was a hot summer day, clouds of dust rising from the horse's hooves. And then he was in the mud again, his face pushed deep, and his body numb, beginning to be cold again. He struggled to get up, sensing his danger. But he slipped back down, and then he was back on the horse, and the sky around him was blue, without any clouds.

He was fighting to get up again, afraid of the summer and the sky he had seen. "Help me! Help me!" He was on his feet, staggering up the shore, because he knew he was beyond the fires. "Help me!" He could not see. All was black, but he knew which way he had to go and he walked as best he could. He would have to climb the steep bluff that was there somewhere, and he knew without a doubt that he could not do it. But he intended to try. He kept walking, knowing the fires were above the bank, realizing that he couldn't see them from the foot of the bluff. He didn't even know how far he had to go.

He kept going, however, until he stumbled and fell onto his hands and knees. It seemed that he couldn't get up. "Help!" he screamed, with all the voice he had, but hardly anything came out. "Help! Help!" He waited and took a breath and yelled again, but he was hardly whispering.

"Who's down there?" someone said.

Joseph couldn't answer. He tried to get up and slipped onto his chest.

"Who's down there?"

"Help me," Joseph gasped.

"What? What did you say?"

"Help me, help me." But no one could have heard him.

And then someone was near him—faster than he thought possible—and Joseph didn't know how he had gotten over on his back.

"Who are you?" The world was spinning, and a dark face

was caught, fixed, in the middle, above his own face. "Who are you?"

"Joseph Williams. Far West."

After a time there were more people, and Joseph realized he was being carried, except that sometimes he was back on his horse in the summer, with the sky all around him. "He's half froze," someone said. "We've got to get him warm."

When Joseph understood where he was the next time, he was in a cabin. His clothes had been taken off, and he was wrapped in a blanket. A man was saying "Brother Williams, how did you get here? How did you get in the river?"

Joseph couldn't think of an answer. The right answer was too big right now. He went to sleep.

Chapter 8

When Joseph awoke the next day, he was confused. He couldn't remember where he was. But then he saw Joseph Smith sitting at the table, talking to Brother Hinkle. "Brother Joseph."

The Prophet got up and walked to the bed where Joseph was lying. "How are you feeling?"

"All right, I guess." But he felt weak, and his feet and hands ached. He wanted to go back to sleep.

"Why did you come here?" the Prophet asked. He was bending over Joseph, speaking gently.

"Brother Hyrum sent me. He didn't know what was happening. He was afraid you needed help and couldn't send for it."

"I see. How did you get here? They said you came out of the river, almost frozen."

"I stole a boat. But I didn't have an oar. I got in as close as I could, and then I swam for it."

"Oh, Joseph." The Prophet sat down on the bed and touched the boy's shoulder. "It's a miracle you made it in that water. It was a brave thing to do."

"Was it all right—I mean, taking the boat that way?"

Joseph Smith didn't answer at first, and Joseph was afraid of what he might say. The Prophet looked terribly tired, and his face seemed thinner than usual. There was a sadness in his eyes that reminded Joseph of the day in Clay County when the men of Zion's Camp were dying of cholera. "Joseph, we've been pushed to extremes by this mob we're facing. They're starving us out, killing our animals, shooting at us from the woods. Two of our people died yesterday. They were sick, and we couldn't feed them properly. I think a boat is a small thing by comparison." He sat for some time and said nothing, but Joseph could feel that more was on his mind. "Before this is all over, I hate to think what we might have to do."

Joseph had never heard the Prophet speak this way. "Are we going to start shooting back?"

"We've already returned some of their fire. But it's hopeless. We're outnumbered, and more of their militias are gathering in from all the counties around here. We'd hoped to stall until we could get help from the governor, but Boggs simply says we'll have to fight it out for ourselves. And Brother Hinkle wants to do just that. But I think of the slaughter we'd see here and I can't sanction it." He looked at the floor for a time. "I suppose we'll have to leave. Maybe today. But we can't keep running forever. Someone is going to have to give us room or finally see our wrath."

Neither spoke for quite some time, until Joseph said, "I'm awfully tired, Brother Joseph."

"I know you are, Joseph. I hope you can rest a day or two, but if we are forced to leave today, you'll have to get up and go with us. Do you think you can walk?"

"Sure. I can walk." The Prophet stood up. "But Brother Joseph, I lost my boots and my coat."

Joseph Smith stood still. The light was across one side of his

55

cheek, and Joseph could see that his jaw had tightened, the muscles bulging. "Oh, Joseph," he said. "What am I putting my people through? I can't even promise that I can find boots for you, or a coat. But I'll do my best. You rest now."

Joseph fell asleep, or halfway so. He slept fitfully, his mind full of the cold water and the turbulence of the night before. And in his restlessness, he kept grabbing for his boots, deep under the surface of the black Missouri. The river was powerful in his mind, like a great snake. He wanted his boots and his coat. He wanted to be home working with Matthew in the fields, talking about the good harvest. As he began to wake again, he wondered why he had been so eager to come here.

Joseph Smith had returned and was standing over the bed again. Hours had gone by, and somehow Joseph sensed that, although he hardly felt that he had slept. "Joseph, you'll have to get up. We're going to leave, all of us. We've been promised safe passage out of here. We're going to Far West. There are no coats, but we have some blankets. You'll have to wrap yourself up. It's bitter cold outside. I *was* able to get you these."

He was holding a pair of boots with the toes worn though. They looked much too big. "Thank you," Joseph said, and he sat up.

"See if one of the brethren has some extra stockings he can let you take. Put on as many as you can. I'm sorry we have no better. I'm afraid some of the children are without shoes."

Joseph Smith turned then, apparently about to go. "Brother Joseph."

"Yes."

"My horse is up the river a ways. I need to get her."

"I don't know, Joseph. We'd better stay together."

"But I tied her in the woods. She could die out there."

"Let's talk about it later, Joseph. We'll see what we can do—once we're out of town."

For the next hour or so, everyone was packing up all they could put into wagons or on horseback. Much had to be left behind. Joseph realized he had been staying in an old cabin—just a shack really—where George Hinkle and Lyman Wight had been staying since they had come to DeWitt. But Joseph was taken to another cabin and given a little mush made from boiled corn. It was coarse and tasteless, but afterward he was ashamed that he had eaten so much when he learned that the adults in DeWitt had eaten next to nothing for the last three days.

When the wagon train pulled out of DeWitt, Joseph was wrapped in an old wool blanket. He walked awkwardly in the huge boots. The old settlers lined the road and mocked the Saints as they left. The boys were especially pleased when they saw Joseph, and they teased him as he passed. "What's that, a Injun squaw? She shore has big feet." Joseph looked straight ahead, trying not to acknowledge the boys at all.

As the wagons rolled through the mud, Joseph realized the going would be slow, that it would be a terribly long walk in the old boots. He wanted his horse, but he knew that others were in much greater need. Some were so weak they could hardly walk. Joseph saw one brother holding an older man, saying, "Now, Father, I'll let you try to walk a little ways, but you'll have to get in the wagon soon."

"No, I won't," the older man said. "I won't ride when there's women as old as I am walking. I'll die first."

"But you're sick, Father. You just can't—"

"I'll walk. I'm getting my strength now. You don't have to help me." But the son did continue to help him, and the two trudged along slowly. Joseph felt sick inside, the rough mush having not set well after not eating for so long, but he felt

57

ashamed even to think of himself with so much suffering all around him.

One of the old settlers brought the Saints several sacks of cornmeal, but others jeered at him for doing so. Most of the old settlers were not exactly jubilant, but they looked pleased— satisfied—with what they had accomplished. One man spit a black stream of tobacco juice not far from Joseph's feet, and then he said, "What's the matter, boy? You look a little down in the mouth." He laughed deeply, as though he had said something terribly clever. Two men next to him laughed the same way. Joseph hated them. He could feel his heart beating fast, and he was angry enough to strike out at them, even wanted to. It was not even fear that kept him from doing it. If he could just hurt one of the men, it would be worth it. But he couldn't let down the other Saints who were walking humbly before the enemy, not returning the insults.

Before long the Saints were out on the prairie on the road Joseph had followed on his way to DeWitt. The old settlers were behind now, and the problem was the cold and the wet and the hunger. Joseph was near the front of the wagon train but he could look back and see that most of the Saints were walking. The very small children were up on the wagons, and the women were usually driving the teams, but the men and older children were walking, and many of those children had no shoes. Some had wrapped their feet in rags.

Joseph Smith came along after a time. He too was walking. "Joseph," he said, "how far away is your horse?"

Joseph pointed up the river. "It's that way, only about a mile."

"All right, listen. We need all the horses we can get. Are you strong enough to walk to her and then ride back?"

"Sure. If she's still there. I'm afraid she might have pulled loose."

"You could be right. But go after her. If she's not there, don't spend a lot of time looking around, just walk back to us. You can catch up at the pace we're setting. We've gotten a late start, and it's slow going. We'll never make it to Far West tonight. I need you to find your horse and then get to Far West as fast as you can. We need food and dry blankets, and fresh teams and wagons. Can you do that, Joseph?"

"Yes, I'll go right now."

Joseph Smith grabbed the boy's shoulders, stopping him. "Joseph, we have people dying. Some aren't going to make it as it is. If you can make it to Far West tonight, you will save some lives, I'm sure. Do your best." And then the Prophet placed his hands upon Joseph's head—those big, heavy hands. "In the name of Jesus Christ, I bless you, Joseph Williams," he said. And then, "Lord, protect him and help him to fulfill his calling today."

Joseph was taken aback. He had not expected this. He nodded his thanks, but he could not speak.

"You go now. Hurry," the Prophet said.

Joseph walked hard, even ran at times, in spite of the heavy boots. He reached the river quickly, and he felt fine, but as he began his trek up the river, he realized that everything looked different in the daylight. He was not at all sure where he had left his horse. He would have to walk in the woods to have any chance of finding her.

Unfortunately, this made the going very difficult, the underbrush being so heavy and brittle this time of year. The blanket caught at almost every step. Joseph finally folded it up and carried it in front of him, that being less trouble. But his old shirt was soon torn, and blood trickled from his arms and along his sides. He couldn't worry about that. He had to push through, had to hurry. But he was beginning to realize what he had been through the night before. He was tiring fast.

Before long, however, he did find the clearing, the place where he had left old Molly. He found her tracks, where she had stood and stomped, and where she had paced around the tree. But she had pulled loose and was gone.

Joseph remembered the Prophet's words. He should not spend a lot of time looking for her. But Joseph could see Molly's tracks very clearly in the mud. He decided to follow her at least a little ways and see if he could find her.

She had headed out of the woods away from the river, and onto the prairie. Joseph followed the tracks quite a long way west until he found the place where she had turned back into the woods. He followed through the woods toward the river, and then, as he broke out into a clearing he saw her. She was standing with another horse, by a cabin. It was the ferryman's.

Joseph had no choice. He walked directly to the cabin. He knocked on the door, even though he still wasn't certain what he would say. In a moment a tall man, an old man without any teeth, opened the decaying door. He squinted to see Joseph. "Excuse me, sir. That's my horse. She got away last night. If I could just have the saddle, I'll be gone. Thank you for keeping her for me." Joseph hadn't used his Missouri speech. He had no time to play games.

The man grinned, showing the pink of his gums. "That there's my horse. I don't know what you're talkin' about."

"She came here just this morning. You know that."

"Only thing I know is that last night somebody stold my boat, an' this morning I got me a new horse an' saddle. I figure that the Lord teks an' he gives too. This time things got evened out a little."

"But it's my horse."

"Who er you, anyway?"

Joseph had no patience to go through all this. He needed his horse. "Joseph Williams. I'm from Far West. I'm a Mormon, and our people have been forced out of DeWitt. I need my horse to help them."

The old man grinned again, his eyes becoming red slits filled at the corners with something white and filmy. "How'd yer horse git clear up here?"

"I left her in the woods last night while I went into DeWitt. Now listen, I've got to have that horse right now. I can't stand around here and—"

"Did you tek my boat?"

Joseph stood in front of the man, wondering what to say. He took a breath. "Yes."

The man nodded and smiled. "Leastways yer honest. But you ain't smart. We made a trade. Yer horse and saddle for my boat. Now you git along."

"Sir, I have to have that horse. I'm stronger than you. I can force my way in and take my saddle if I have to. I had to take your boat, but I'll pay you back when I can. You can trust me."

The man laughed a sort of cackle. "First you tell me yer gonna break my head, and then you say I kin trust yuh. I'll tell you what I kin trust." He reached for something.

Joseph lunged and grabbed the man's arm, knocking the rifle to the floor. He then leaped forward and picked it up. "Now where's my saddle?" But Joseph saw it on the floor. He scooped it up with one arm and kept hold of the rifle with the other. He didn't point it at the man, but he kept it handy. He went out then and saddled Molly. The man came out, but he stood back, squinting to see, not saying anything.

Joseph worked as fast as he could. Then he said, "All right, mister. I'm leaving your rifle right here on the ground. I'll be back sometime to pay you for the boat. I'm sorry."

Joseph rode away. He half expected the old man to try to shoot him, but nothing happened. At least he had fed his horse, and she was ready to ride for a while.

Joseph headed back to the road. Within an hour he had caught up with the wagon train, or he thought he had. But then he could see that a couple of the wagons had stopped. A woman was standing by one of the wagons, looking toward the nearby woods. She looked up at Joseph as he approached.

"What's the trouble, Sister?" Joseph asked.

"It's Sister Michaels," the woman said. "She didn't make it. She was weak—from the new baby—and she just couldn't take all this . . ." The woman put her hand to her forehead and began to cry. There were two little children in the wagon. Joseph wondered if they belonged to Sister Michaels, but he didn't ask.

"Are they going to bury her out there?" Joseph said.

The woman nodded, still sobbing. "What a thing," she said. "Just leave her out here like this."

"I'm riding ahead for help," Joseph said. "I'll . . . I'll do what I can. Do you need anything?"

"No, we're fine. You go on ahead. Don't you have a coat?" Now that she had uncovered her face, Joseph could see that she was a young woman—maybe twenty-three or -four. But her face was drawn and thin and terribly pale.

Joseph was feeling cold now. He had lost the blanket in the fuss with the old man. "Well, no," he said. "I had a blanket, but I lost it."

"Here, take a blanket from us. We have plenty," she said. "You'll need it." She went behind the wagon, reached in, and pulled out a blanket, and then brought it back to Joseph.

"I'm grateful to you," Joseph said, "but I can get one when I catch up to the other wagons. You have children and—"

"No, no. We have plenty for our needs. Don't worry about that. Now hurry on."

Joseph felt sorry for her, for Brother Michaels, whom he didn't know, for the children. But he was also angry. Joseph wanted to be there when the big fight came. Someone needed to pay for this.

Joseph caught up with the other wagons, spoke briefly to Joseph Smith, and then hurried on toward Far West. He had not eaten anything except the mush that morning, and by late afternoon he was feeling bone tired and very weak. The clouds cleared away for a time, and the temperature was not too bad, but as the sun angled and evening came on, a chilling breeze picked up again. Joseph wrapped the blanket around himself tightly and forced Molly to keep going. He was afraid he was killing the old horse, but he had to make it to Far West as soon as he could.

It was almost morning when he got there. He had rested Molly a couple of times, but he had pushed her beyond what was reasonable. He was numb with cold and exhaustion when he rode into town. He could hardly think. But he stopped at Hyrum Smith's place, not far from his own. He was barely able to stand up. He told Brother Hyrum what had happened and what was needed, and then he led his horse down the street to his home. She was wheezing and resisting, not wanting to take another step.

When he got home he found the latch fastened. He knocked. "Matthew, Mother. It's Joseph." In a moment the door came open. "Matthew," Joseph said, "can you do something for Molly? She's not doing very well." Joseph stepped through the door and then sank to his knees.

Chapter 9

Joseph had something to eat, and then, briefly, he described to Matthew and Mother what had happened. He told them he had had to take the boat, but he didn't mention the forceful way he had taken his horse back. He felt uneasy about that, but he wasn't ready to think about it yet, let alone talk about it. He went to bed and slept until after noon, and he was still very tired when he got up. It was late in the day when the DeWitt party finally made its way into Far West. Wagons had left soon after Joseph had gotten the word to Hyrum Smith, taking food and supplies.

Joseph and Ruth walked to the town square to see the arrival. It was a pitiful sight, and Ruth was shocked. The children, especially, were pale and big-eyed, apparently confused by all they had experienced. Everyone was thin and weak looking. "Look, Joseph," Ruth said. An older woman was being helped from a wagon. She was so weak she couldn't walk. A younger man, maybe her son, carried her to the Rigdon home, just across from the square. Brother Rigdon had a large, double-log house, and many of the sick were being taken there. All the people were being taken in, as much as possible, by the Saints of Far West.

"Why do they all look so sick?" Ruth asked.

"They were starved out, Ruth. They had very little food at the last. And now they've been two days on the road, most of them walking."

"But why?"

Joseph looked down at Ruth. He knew what she was asking was too big for him to answer. It was what he had asked his father back in Jackson County. He didn't say anything, but inside he felt a strange mixture of anger and sadness.

Eventually Joseph spotted the Prophet. He was helping to get the families into homes, walking along the wagons, conferring with people as he went. Joseph stepped up to him as he came by. "Joseph," the Prophet said, "thank you so much for sending the help. Lives were saved because of it." He looked down at Ruth, recognizing how overwhelmed she was. "I'm sorry you have to see this," he said, and he knelt in front of her, taking her hand.

"Why did they want to starve them?" she asked. Her face was flushed from the cold and the emotion, but her eyes were like hollow orbs, round and wide and intense.

"It's not easy to explain," the Prophet said. "They fear us. They think we want their land. And they don't like our religion. But Ruth . . . " He hesitated, still on one knee, looking into Ruth's face. "Not all people are bad. Remember that. We can't let ourselves get all filled up with hate."

Joseph could see that Ruth wasn't satisfied. But the Prophet left it at that. He stood up and looked at Joseph for a moment, as though he wanted to say something else, but then he only said, "Can you take a family into your home?"

"I'm sure we can," Joseph said.

"You'd better run home and ask your mother. They have five children."

"All right. I'll ask her."

Joseph Smith took one step away, and then he stopped and turned back. He pulled Ruth close to him, held her head against his chest. "I'm sorry," he said. "I'm sorry to put you through this, little one. I hope you won't have to see any more of it."

Ruth was crying now, and Joseph was almost glad to see her find release. The Prophet stepped back and smoothed Ruth's hair, and then he walked away. Joseph put his arms around his sister and she sobbed again. "The children didn't even have any shoes," she said. There was nothing to do or say. Joseph only held her.

"Wait here for a minute," he finally said. "I've got to run and ask Mother." Ruth wiped her eyes and stepped back, and Joseph hurried down the street to his house. But he met his mother halfway. She had Samuel with her, and she was walking toward the town square.

"Joseph," she said, "how are they?"

"Well, they made it. But some of them look awfully weak."

"Can we help?"

"That's what I was coming to ask you. Brother Joseph wants us to take in a family of seven people."

"Seven?"

Joseph nodded. His mother looked troubled.

"Yes," she finally said. "We'll manage some way or another."

"Mother, I could ask the prophet if there's a smaller family, maybe someone who—"

"No, Joseph, we'll manage. Go get them. I'll go back and start a meal for them."

"But, Mother, there must be some smaller families."

"No. I want this chance." She sounded firm, like Matthew, or even Father. "Joseph, I'm scared. You know that. But I'll do my part. We all have to do that."

66

And so Joseph went back and told the Prophet.

"All right," Joseph Smith said. "Just walk down to your house. Brother Engbert is going to drive the wagon and follow you." He shook the boy's hand. "Thank you, Joseph," he said. He seemed to mean more than just thanks for taking in the family.

Joseph walked home, with Ruth alongside. And when they arrived, Mother came out to greet the Engberts. They got down from the wagon and came in the house. Brother Engbert was carrying a baby wrapped in a blanket. He was a fairly big man, who had once been rather heavy, it seemed. Now the skin hung loose along his jaws and throat. Sister Engbert looked gaunt, and somehow too old to have such a little baby. There were three daughters, one maybe older than Joseph, and the other two younger. They were not pretty girls. They looked tired and dirty, and their hair hung in matted strings. There was also a little boy, about seven or eight, whose lips looked blue against his white skin.

Sister Williams had them all come to the fire. They crowded around silently. Brother Engbert said, "Thank you so much, Sister Williams," but that was all.

The baby whimpered a bit, and then the young boy began to cry. One of the daughters, the middle one, knelt down and put her arms around him, which seemed only to bring on deeper sobs. "My fingers hurt," he said.

Sister Williams spent the week making clothes for the Engbert girls and looking after the baby and little boy, who were both sick. Joseph and Matthew spent their days completing the harvest, and after a couple of days, Brother Engbert helped them. But the boys were finding that selling their corn was not easy. Not only was there a surplus because of good crops, but many old settlers refused to deal with Mormons. And when the Saints took their corn to be ground for their own use, they were turned down at the mills they had always used. Some of the Mormon-owned mills had been abandoned because of the harassment the outlying settlements were receiving. The Williamses still had some meal left, but it was not going to last long with twelve people eating it.

What was an even greater worry was that troubles had begun again in Daviess County, and ugly incidents were being reported almost daily. Most of the Saints who lived away from Diahman had now been driven out of their homes. Lyman Wight reported that a battle could start at any moment. General Parks was sent in to quiet matters, but most of his troops sided with the old settlers. He warned the Saints that they had to be prepared to defend themselves. And things were now almost as bad in Caldwell County. Many of the Saints moved into Far West, guards were stationed about the city, and all-out war seemed at hand.

On Sunday Joseph Smith gave a powerful sermon, calling on the Saints to look out for each other and to defend themselves against the tyrannical mobs who wanted to drive them from their land. He quoted the scripture, "Greater love hath no man than this, that he lay down his life for his brethren." And then at the end he asked that all who would stand by him and defend the kingdom of God gather at the town square in the morning.

Joseph came away feeling ready to do what had to be done. He would get a gun somewhere, and he would go offer himself to the militia. They needed him now, and they could hardly turn him down. But at the meeting the next morning Matthew volunteered to ride with the militia to Daviess County again. Joseph knew that this time the problems there could be much more severe, and he also knew that it was not time to give his mother further worry. He said nothing about his intention to join the militia, but when the battle came to Far West, or if it did, Joseph wanted to be part of it.

It was a long week, with little news from Diahman, or from Joseph Smith. Joseph continued to harvest the corn, but on Wednesday morning it began to snow. It was an early storm, but a heavy and wet one. It left Joseph relatively idle for the next couple of days and gave him more time to worry. Mother was now boiling the corn, and she and the Engbert girls were grinding it with a bowl and pestle and with a piece of tin that had holes punched in it. But it was a gritty meal that was very unpleasant to eat. Joseph had killed some chickens to give the Engberts a little meat that week, and there was a fairly good supply of potatoes and pumpkins and turnips, but cornbread was the staple for people who lived on the prairies, and Joseph felt it would be a long winter if he couldn't find a way to get some of their corn ground.

On Thursday afternoon, as the snow was beginning to melt, Joseph loaded his wagon with corn and drove to the mill where he had always gone. But it was no use. As soon as the owner saw him, he came to Joseph and told him he had better clear out before some of the men realized he was a Mormon and made things unpleasant—not just for Joseph but for the mill owner himself. Joseph was enraged, but he didn't say anything. He simply turned his wagon around and left. The man had always been happy to have Joseph's business up until now. What a coward he was. Joseph remembered what the Prophet had said about the Saints not giving themselves up to hatred, and he knew the Prophet was right, but it was one thing to believe he shouldn't hate and quite another actually to control what he was feeling. For the moment he wasn't even sure he wanted the struggle—there was a certain satisfaction in hatred. It was better than nothing.

Chapter 10

Matthew was gone for a week. When he came back, he said that he thought maybe matters were under control in Daviess County, but he would not say much more than that. He looked tired. Joseph and he went out to the fields that afternoon, and Matthew praised Joseph for managing so well without him, but his voice lacked conviction. Joseph tried to find out more about what had happened, but Matthew fended off every question, and finally he told Joseph not to ask.

And so Joseph and Matthew worked together that next week, saying little to each other. They slept in the loft alongside Samuel and Ruth, since the Engberts took up much of the house, sleeping on blankets on the floor. Joseph didn't resent the Engberts' presence, but the demand was considerable on his mother, and they were also a constant reminder that things were not well.

On Thursday, not long after everyone had settled down to sleep, someone knocked at the door. "Who is it?" Mother said.

"Sister Williams, I need to talk to Matthew," the voice said. Matthew got up quickly, pulled on his trousers, and climbed down the ladder. He stepped out into the cold and asked what

70

was wanted. Joseph was lying on the floor of the loft, near the front of the cabin. He could hear Matthew just outside and below him. And he heard the other voice.

"There's trouble down south of here. Some of our people were taken captive by that crazy minister, Bogart. He's leading a mob down there that he calls a militia. We're organizing to go free the captives."

There was a long silence and Joseph thought that Matthew had spoken too softly to be heard in the loft. But then he heard Matthew say, "I won't be able to go this time. I've gone twice. I need to catch up on things here now."

"Matthew," the voice said, "I don't think you can do that. The Sons of Dan won't put up with it."

"I told you, I can't go."

"But Matthew, if I tell Captain Avard, it's hard to say what he might—"

"That's all right. I'll worry about that. I can't go. If we're attacked here, I'll fight with the militia."

"All right, Matthew. But I wouldn't want to be in your shoes. Captain Avard won't forget this."

Then Matthew came back in the house and climbed the ladder again. Mother asked him what it was about. "Nothing very important," he said, and then he went back to bed. Joseph lay awake long after that, and he could tell that Matthew was awake too. Joseph couldn't understand. This was not at all like Matthew. Joseph felt a little ashamed for him, and yet he knew there had to be some explanation. Joseph knew something had happened to Matthew in Daviess County.

The next morning Matthew and Joseph and Brother Engbert got up early and went out to the farm. Joseph waited until he and Matthew were alone, and then he asked Matthew what the man had wanted the night before.

"It's nothing to concern you, Joseph," Matthew said.

"When some of our members are taken prisoner by a mob, that concerns me," Joseph said.

Matthew had been getting ready to harness the mules, but now he stopped, still holding a collar in his hands. "What else did you hear?"

"Everything you said. And I don't understand. We don't have *that* much to do right now. You could have gone."

Matthew was putting on his hard exterior, his face screening all emotion. "We have plenty to do—this field to plow under, and those hogs to kill and butcher and salt."

"That could wait a few days yet."

Matthew looked stern, but his eyes revealed a certain confusion. "Joseph, you cannot possibly understand the whole situation. And I can't tell you any more than I have. You'll have to trust me."

"I want to, Matthew. But you won't explain anything. You'll hardly talk. Who are the Sons of Dan?"

"Joseph, I can't tell you. And you have got to promise me never to mention them again."

"Why?"

"Joseph, just promise me. It's *very* important."

"What's going on, Matthew? I don't see why—"

"Joseph, listen to me!" He grabbed Joseph's shoulders. "You've just got to trust me for now. I'm doing what I think is best. But you must promise me never to speak of the Danites again."

"The Danites?"

"The Sons of Dan."

"But tell me who they are, and then I'll promise."

"I can't, Joseph. I simply can't."

"Something's wrong with you, Matthew. You've changed lately. You're—"

"I don't care what it seems, Joseph. Just consider me a coward if you want to, but promise me you won't mention the Danites to anyone."

"All right." Joseph didn't like it, but he simply gave in.

Matthew dropped his hands, and the two stood looking at each other. Matthew seemed in some sort of pain, in spite of his attempt to cover it up. Joseph wanted to understand, wanted even to help if he could. And beneath it all, he did trust Matthew. But he hated the very suggestion of weakness in his brother. Matthew had always been his strength.

Joseph plowed, and Matthew and Brother Engbert killed two hogs, bled them, skinned them, and split them in half. They hung them in the barn before walking back to town that afternoon. Joseph and Matthew went to Lightner's store to see if they could hear what news had come back to Far West from the group that had gone south during the night. Some men were standing inside the store, at the front, when the boys came in.

"Have you heard what's happened to the men who went after Bogart last night?" Matthew asked.

Brother Judd turned around. "Yes, Brother Williams, I'm afraid we have. It was a bad business. Some of our people are dead. Apostle Patten, for one."

"David Patten is dead?"

"Yes, and so is Gideon Carter. And there's others that's dying. There's a boy by the name of O'Bannion—they say he'll never live. And Brother Hendricks was shot through the neck. I don't know if he'll make it or not."

"What happened, exactly?" Matthew asked. Joseph could see that Matthew was taking this hard. His hands were shaking.

"Well, no one knows for sure. I guess our boys found Bogart camped along the Crooked River somewhere. They went in before the sun was even up and tried to take them by surprise. There was shooting, and I guess we killed some of them too, but no one knows yet how many it was."

"Did we get our prisoners back?"

"Yes," Brother Judd said, "I guess we did do that."

"It's an awful high price to pay," another of the men said. "Brother Patten was as good a man as I know."

"He was brave," Joseph said. "He wasn't scared of anything." Joseph glanced at Matthew, who was looking down at the floor. Suddenly Joseph felt angry that his brother hadn't been there. Joseph would have gone himself, had he had the chance.

The boys left after that, but they had hardly gotten outside when Joseph said, "Well, Matthew, how do you feel now?" Joseph was tired of the silence; he wanted to force Matthew to explain, even if he had to make him angry to do it.

Matthew gave Joseph one hard look, full of coldness and controlled anger, and then he began to walk fast.

"You should have been there, Matthew. Aren't you even ashamed?"

Matthew kept walking, hard. Joseph, even with his long legs, had to hurry to keep up. "Joseph, don't say that again. Don't talk to me at all."

"But it's true, Matthew. I would have gone. I wish I *could* have gone!"

Matthew spun then and grabbed Joseph by the arm. For a moment Joseph thought Matthew was going to swing at him. "Joseph, you are not going to get involved in any of this. You are not going to be in the militia. If there's trouble here in Far West, you will stay home. Do you understand that?"

"No. I'm ready to fight. And I will. You won't see me lose my nerve either. You be the preacher, Matthew, and let me do the fighting. It'll be better that way."

Matthew's grip tightened, not in fury, but with power. "Joseph, don't ever talk that way to me again. Do you hear me? I'll give up my life to protect you and Mother and the little ones, if that's what I have to do. But I won't do what is against my conscience."

"What do you mean, Matthew?"

"Just what I said. And it's all I'm going to say. I wish I had gone to Crooked River and gotten myself shot—if that's what it takes to make you proud of me. But *you* will not go to battle. You will look after Mother. That's how it must be, Joseph; that's how it *will* be. I want to save the farm. I want to live here. I want Mother and Ruth and Samuel to be safe and happy. I want to keep the promises I made to Father. But if I'm killed, you'll have to keep the promises. I'm not asking you, Joseph. I'm telling you!"

Joseph didn't argue. He knew better. And in a way he was satisfied. Matthew's vision of what had to be had always carried the family through since Father died. Joseph was accustomed to seeing things through Matthew's eyes. And there was a certain force behind what Matthew had said. He hadn't exactly answered Joseph, but Joseph was reassured. Matthew was no coward, and the truth was, Joseph had known that all along.

In the next few days, more of the story about the battle at Crooked River came out. Only one of Bogart's men had been killed, but several had been wounded. Patrick O'Bannion died; however, the others in the Mormon company were surviving. But throughout the counties in western Missouri, the rumors were spreading fast that the Mormons had risen up and massacred the Ray County militia and that now the Mormons were in open rebellion against the state, ready to kill anyone who got in their way. Armies were being readied in every county in western Missouri. There seemed no question now that a war was about to begin.

Chapter 11

Saturday David Patten was buried. It was October 27. The weather had returned to normal for that time of year, not being quite so cold. Almost everyone in Far West turned out for the funeral, including the many who had been forced into town from outlying settlements. Joseph Smith preached an impressive sermon, admonishing the Saints not to give way to despair. The members seemed buoyed up afterward, but their grief for Apostle Patten was deep. He had been much loved, perhaps more than any of the leaders, except for the Prophet.

After the ceremony the Williamses and the Engberts walked back to town together, the cemetery being on the prairie just outside Far West. Joseph had gradually come to know the names of the Engbert girls, but he paid little attention to them. Carla was the oldest. She was a stout girl with a rather stiff manner and a harsh face. She hardly ever said anything. The younger girl, Malinda, looked much the same but was a little more talkative. But Mary Ann, who was just a few months younger than Joseph, was more to Joseph's liking. She wasn't particularly pretty, not like Emily Cox, but she was a straightforward person, and friendly, and when she smiled, she actually looked quite nice.

There had not been much call for smiling lately, but she had been fairly cheerful and a constant help to her mother and to Sister Williams. But what Joseph liked best about her was that she was angry, and she didn't mind saying so. She didn't pardon the old settlers for what they had done in DeWitt. Joseph had heard her say she would like to take her pa's rifle and make things hot for a few of those people. Old Missourians would have said that she had some grit in her, and Joseph thought that was all right.

Joseph was walking along carrying Samuel on his shoulders. Mary Ann was beside him, not totally by accident, at least on Joseph's part. "Did you know Brother Patten?" Mary Ann asked.

"Sure I did."

"Was he as good a man as everyone said, or was that just funeral talk?" And she was serious.

Joseph laughed. It was the first time he had laughed in some time. "He was an apostle, wasn't he?"

"That doesn't mean that much," she said, smiling just a little. "Some of those men think they're a little too holy, if you ask me. Especially Brother Rigdon."

Joseph laughed so loudly that his mother turned around and shushed him. "Brother Rigdon's not so bad," Joseph said, but he was still laughing, although more quietly, and Samuel had begun to giggle, as though the sheer joy of hearing laughter again was a delight to him. "You have to be around him some. But Brother Patten was the best. Everyone liked him. And he was brave. He didn't just *talk* brave—like you. He really *was* brave."

Joseph was grinning at her, and she smiled back. Joseph thought she looked better today than she ever had before. "I guess I could take care of myself if I had to," Mary Ann said. "And I don't see you out there drilling with the militia. Maybe *I'll* have to fight, if the men won't. Or the *boys*—like you."

Joseph had gotten into a little battle he couldn't win. She had knocked a hole in his armor with the very first blow. Joseph didn't say much for a time, though he tried not to show his reaction. Mary Ann seemed to know she had won, but she didn't back off a bit. She teased him about being tall, but too skinny, without any muscles. "Now, Matthew—he's the one with muscles," she said. "And he's handsome too."

This second blow was perhaps even harder than the first. Joseph felt his ears get hot, and for the life of him he couldn't think of anything to say. Fortunately, little Samuel said, "Mary Ann, do you want to marry Maffew?" That seemed to embarrass even Mary Ann, and she was more quiet the rest of the way home.

The next day at church Joseph heard the rumors that were spreading. Some of the Saints were clearing out, afraid of what was coming. Even some of the leaders had joined with the dissenters and were slipping away from Far West. Thomas Marsh and Orson Hyde, both apostles, had gone. And Joseph was especially disappointed to learn that John Corrill, who had been through all the difficulties in Jackson and Clay, was now denouncing the Prophet for leading them into disaster by resisting the authority of the state. This didn't make sense to Joseph. The "authority" was the mob—the so-called militias—which had no right to push the Saints off their lands. It was painful, even frightening to see dissension and bickering among the very leaders of the Church.

* * *

On Tuesday Joseph and Matthew were repairing their little log barn, getting it ready for the severe cold to come. Early in the afternoon, a man on horseback came toward them. He was riding hard. "Brother Williams," he shouted as he reined up his horse, "the militia's being called up. An army is marching toward Far West, from the south."

Joseph felt his breath catch. For several days now there had been little doubt that this was coming, and Joseph had vowed not to be scared, but he suddenly felt the cold penetrate him. This was it. The old settlers had actually decided to attack Far West, where thousands of Mormons lived. Somehow it had always seemed that it couldn't come to this.

Joseph turned to Matthew as the rider spurred his horse, but just then the man reined the horse back again and twisted in the saddle. "Are you Joseph?" He shouted. Joseph nodded. "Brother Hyrum wants to see you—just as fast as you can get to his house!"

Matthew and Joseph put their tools away quickly. "Joseph," Matthew said, "I don't know what Brother Hyrum wants you to do. But as soon as you've taken care of it, get back to Mother and the others. Brother Engbert hasn't drilled with us, but I'm sure he'll want to help. We'll have to depend on you to look after the women and children."

"But what could I do, Matthew? I don't have a weapon—not anything."

"Joseph, I'm not talking about fighting. Keep everyone calm. Take care of their needs. Keep them in food. And if our army loses, somehow you'll have to bring them through it all. But don't go looking for a gun. You'll get yourself killed, and then you won't be any help to anyone."

"But are they actually going to attack us?"

"I don't know, Joseph. They aren't marching up here for the pleasure of it."

Matthew went home and got his gun and headed to the city square. Joseph stopped long enough to tell his mother what he had to do, and then he hurried down the street to Hyrum

80

Smith's. He found Hyrum out in front, talking to several men. "Joseph," he said, "we need your help. Do you know the way to Haun's Mill?

"Sure I do."

"All right. We want you to ride there as fast as you can. My horse is ready, and we've packed some food for you. Most of the Saints in outlying settlements have already come in to Far West, but Jacob Haun decided to keep his people where they were. They need to know what's happening. I think they'd better come here, if it's not too late."

"How close is the army, Brother Hyrum?

"We're not exactly sure. If they keep marching, we understand they'll be here by sundown. Can you leave right now, Joseph? You need to make it there before dark yourself."

"Yes, I can leave now. But could you talk to my mother? She hates to be alone right now."

"All right. I can do that. The horse is out back. And listen, Joseph, don't take any chances. Don't try to come back tonight. You could be fired upon out there in the dark where soldiers can't see that you're a boy."

Joseph agreed to that, and then he hurried to the horse. He was happy to have something to do—not to sit home and wait. He headed down the Salem road, which angled to the southeast. He scanned the hills on the southern horizon. There were patches of snow across the browning prairies, and woods covered the more distant hills. He wondered where the army was, how soon it would arrive in Far West. He suddenly shuddered. What would he find when he got back?

* * *

Joseph was tired when he approached Shoal Creek, where Haun's Mill was located. He had ridden steadily all afternoon,

81

and now it was almost sunset. As he approached the little settlement, he could see the mill and the six houses, all built near the
trees along the creek. There were also some pitched tents and
some covered wagons near the blacksmith shop. He could see
people moving about, and it struck him that there was something strange about their behavior. Several people, mostly
women, seemed to be crouching by the blacksmith shop, and
then one woman stood up and ran to Jacob Haun's house, which
was close by. Two women had just picked something up, something heavy, and they were struggling with it, trying to carry it
somewhere. Suddenly Joseph realized what it was. It was a man
they were carrying. At the same moment another woman stood
up and pointed toward Joseph. She yelled something that Joseph
couldn't make out, and in a moment a man came out of the
blacksmith shop and pointed a rifle in Joseph's direction.

"Don't shoot," Joseph yelled. "I'm from Far West." By now
they could hear him. The man dropped the gun to his side.
Joseph kicked his horse and hurried toward them. But now he
was beginning to understand. He could see what the kneeling
women were tending to. There were men on the ground—
bodies.

Joseph could hardly breathe. The man with the gun was staring at him, and the two women had to put down the body they
were trying to move. The others were looking up from where
they were kneeling. Everyone was looking at him, but blankly,
hopelessly. Their faces were stern, wide-eyed, full of shock.

"What happened?" Joseph said as he got down from his
horse, but no one answered. A man on the ground groaned and
the woman by him turned back to him. He was shot through the
leg. Blood was spilling through his torn trousers, just above the
knee. The woman began cutting away the woolen fabric.

Joseph looked back to the man with the rifle. His face was

ashen, and his eyes were still locked on Joseph. Blood was dripping from his hand. The muscles under his eyes, and beneath his black beard, seemed to be twitching, or maybe he was gritting his teeth. "Who are you?" he asked.

"I'm Joseph Williams. Brother Hyrum sent me to . . ." There was nothing to say now. Joseph looked around again, trying to comprehend. He could hear some terrible braying, the cows in the nearby fields all bellowing at once, and dogs were howling mournfully. A woman was crying, the sound seeming to come from the Blacksmith shop. "What happened?" Joseph said again.

"Look inside," the man said, pointing at the shop. It wasn't chinked well, and Joseph could see between the logs. He could see two women inside. The logs were pitted and torn on the outside with hundreds of bullet holes. He walked to the door and looked in. But he had to look away almost immediately. The floor was heaped with bodies, several men lying across each other, and the blood was running in a little river toward the door, dripping onto the single step. The women were holding each other, both sobbing.

Joseph spun around, but then he saw the boy. He was little, not more than nine or ten, and he was lying in the dust, his body having been laid out straight. His coat had been placed over his face. And now the coat was filled with blood, the stain, dark red, almost black, oozing into the dust. Joseph was shaking, too shocked to feel much pain yet, but he pulled his arms in against his quivering sides and stared at the little body. "Why?"

"Can you help me?" someone said, a woman. Joseph turned around and saw that the woman who had been dressing the wounded man's leg was looking at him. "I've put something of a bandage on Brother Foutz's wound. Can you help him into the house?"

Joseph hurried over and then helped him to his feet. He took much of the man's weight on his shoulders as they walked to Brother Haun's house. "Thank you," Brother Foutz said. "Thank you." His voice was thick, and he grunted with each step on the wounded leg.

"Who did it?" Joseph asked.

"Comstock. Jennings. From Livingston County over here. There were two hundred of them—maybe more."

"Why?"

Brother Foutz didn't say anything. Joseph had not really expected an answer. They struggled through the door and then found that several others were already there, lying on the floor. A man was groaning, almost screaming. He was on his side, curled up against the pain that seemed to be in his stomach.

A woman was kneeling by a child, an even smaller boy. Tears were running down her face, but she was not crying aloud. "Brother Foutz. I thought you were dead too." Her voice squeezed off, but she nodded to him, seemingly wanting to say more.

"I was there when they did it, Sister Smith," Foutz said. "There was nothing I could do. They only left me because they thought I was dead. I'm so sorry."

She nodded again. "I know," she said. And then she broke down. She covered her face with her hands.

Brother Foutz whispered to Joseph, "They killed her husband. And that's her little boy out there with the top of his head shot off."

Joseph helped Brother Foutz get down to the floor. Then he took off his coat and put it under Brother Foutz's head. "Why?" he whispered. "Why did they shoot a little boy?"

"Some of us ran for the blacksmith shop. We thought it would make something of a fort. But the gaps in the logs were too wide. They shot through them, and all our men started to

84

fall." He stopped to breathe, and his eyes shut momentarily. "I got hit in the leg and went down. Then Brother Lewis told everyone to run for it, that we would all be killed in there. Those who could, ran, but I had to stay. So I pulled some of the men over on me, and I acted like I was dead." He took a breath again. "When the shooting stopped, some of Jennings's men came in. They didn't notice me, but they found little Sardius hiding under the bellows. I didn't even realize he was there." Tears welled up in Brother Foutz's eyes. "They took him out and . . ."

"That's all right," Joseph said. "Don't talk."

"One of the men said, 'Don't shoot him. He's just a boy.' But then another one said, 'Yes, and nits will make lice.' He fired his pistol right into the boy's head. I didn't know until after, but they had killed the Merrick boy too—when he tried to run from the shop. He was about the same age. His father's also dead."

Joseph stood up. He looked around him. "What can I do?" he said, not knowing whom to ask. He realized he was crying, that tears were dripping from his chin. He needed to do something, help someone.

A man in the corner, sitting up, spoke. "I'm Jacob Haun." Joseph hadn't recognized him. His face was swollen and his eyes were drawn deep. "Can you look about in the woods along the creek? Some of the wounded ran for their lives. I'm afraid they might be bleeding to death, just lying out there."

"Shouldn't he go back to Far West?" It was Sister Smith. "We need help."

"He can't ride now. It's getting dark. It's too dangerous. He'll have to head back in the morning."

"But we need help, Brother Haun. We need a doctor. We need medicine. My little Alma is in terrible pain."

Joseph looked down at the boy. The wound was in his hip.

But he showed no sign of pain at the moment. He seemed to be sleeping. He was so little. Joseph thought of Samuel.

"Brother Haun," Joseph said, "an army is marching toward Far West. By now the Saints might have been attacked."

Brother Haun's eyes opened wide for the first time. "What will we ever do?" he said. Sister Smith began to sob again. The man who was shot in the stomach continued his terrible groaning.

Joseph wished desperately that he could help. "I'll go now," he said. "I can be back to Far West by midnight. Maybe someone can still come."

"No. No, not until morning," Haun said, resolutely. "I want no more boys killed this day."

"But—"

"No. Go out and help. Find something to cover poor Brother McBride with. He's on the ground outside the shop and toward the creek a ways. And then walk into the woods and call out. Try to see if you can help anyone who's still hiding."

Joseph went outside. He took the blanket he had brought with him, tied to his horse, and he walked toward the creek, past Sardius Smith. He found the body—Brother McBride. He was lying on his back. Joseph felt his insides convulse. He turned away for a moment, and then he turned back and quickly spread the blanket over him. He stood for a time, stunned. A woman came up to his side. "They hacked him up," she said. "With a corn-knife. And he was seventy years old. They even stole his boots."

Joseph had to get away. He went to the creek and followed it away from the people and the smell. He wanted to vomit, but he couldn't do it. His insides were gripping with little convulsions. He took hold of a tree, pushed his face against the bark, and then he cried. He shut his eyes and could see the deep red

86

running in the dust, the terrible blackness over everything. He had never bumped up against such a wall of despair. But his tears shut off too soon, leaving him without the relief he had hoped for. He needed to call out, as Brother Haun had told him to do, but he couldn't speak.

Chapter 12

Joseph was able to find no one in the woods, and as night settled in, he gave up the attempt. He went back and told Brother Haun, and then he went to another of the houses where he lay upon the floor all night, not sleeping for a moment. The scenes ran through his mind over and over. Gradually, however, the fear and the horror evolved into other emotions. By morning he was alive with anger, trembling with desire to retaliate. He wanted to get back to Far West. He wanted to get a gun.

He ate a little mush that a sister gave him and he spoke with Brother Haun before he left. Brother Haun said his people would have to bury their dead in the well, that there was not enough time, not enough men, to dig graves. He told Joseph to hurry. "But be careful," he said. "Don't try to get into Far West if it puts you in danger. We'll have to manage the best we can if help can't be sent to us."

Joseph promised to do his best. But he didn't look around the room. The smell of vomit was in the air, and Joseph was feeling sick again. What he wanted now was anger. There was a kind of solace in it that was so much better than the anguish he had felt the night before. He got out of the house and galloped his horse for most of the first mile. He knew that was a mistake, but he needed to push, needed to get some miles behind him. He wanted to be there when the fight started.

Three hours went by. Joseph pushed the horse as hard as he dared, and he stayed with the road. The way was slightly longer, but he could make the best time on solid footing. He hoped that in two more hours he could be in Far West. But as he came over a little rise, he saw riders, ten or twelve of them, galloping their horses to the north, about to cross the road. He reined up his horse and for a moment couldn't think what to do. They were at the crest of the next hill, maybe a quarter of a mile away. Most of them were wearing blue coats, more or less matching. They were obviously part of a militia. He kicked his horse and turned quickly into a little patch of sumac along the side of the road. He jumped down and led the horse under the tallest of the low trees. It was cover, but only barely enough.

Joseph stayed down for a time, hoping that he hadn't been seen and that the riders were gone. But they weren't. They had stopped on the hill, just north of the road. Joseph ducked back down. He didn't know whether they had seen him, but it didn't seem so. The men had gotten down from their horses and they were not looking toward the thicket of sumac. Joseph waited awhile and then peeked out again. The men were letting their horses graze, and some of the men were sitting down. But why at the top of a hill, in the wind? And then Joseph realized what they must be doing. They had chosen the spot as a lookout. They had been sent to watch the road. Or at least that was the only idea that made sense to Joseph. But now what was he to do? He was trapped.

For now, Joseph decided to wait them out a bit and see whether they hadn't stopped simply to take a rest and let the horses feed. But most of an hour went by and they were showing no sign of moving on. Joseph's anxiety, just waiting, was almost more than he could stand. And Brother Hyrum's horse wanted to move to deeper grass under the lower trees. Joseph knew he had to do something.

His only chance was to leave his cover and get back over the hill, away from the sight of the men. Then he could ride south and eventually loop around, back to the road. He might very well be spotted, but if he stayed where he was, he could be stuck there until nightfall—and night brought other dangers. The only other alternative was to come out on the road and casually ride past the men. He could lie to them if they stopped him. But if they doubted him, they would probably take him prisoner. Or maybe worse. He thought of Sardius Smith.

And so he led the horse out of the thicket and hurried over the top of the hill, heading back to the east. As soon as he was over the top, he mounted the horse and rode down the hill, and then he turned southward through the valley. Eventually he stopped and listened. He could hear no riders behind him. It seemed safe to walk the horse.

But then he did hear riders, coming fast down the valley. It didn't seem to be all of them, maybe two or three. Joseph kicked his horse and bolted ahead for a few strides, but he quickly realized that he would never outrun them on his tired horse. He pushed the horse ahead anyway until he found a place where he could get through to the little creek that ran down the valley. He crossed over and then jumped down. He ran into a thicket of hazel under the willow trees, leading the horse. He tripped and fell and then scrambled up and found a place that seemed mostly blocked from view. Then he stood perfectly still and hoped that the horse would do the same.

The riders were farther behind than he had thought. But they were still coming. Joseph patted the horse, trying to keep it calm, and then he froze as the riders went by. There were only two of them. Joseph didn't get a very good look at them, but he did see that one of them had a rifle in his hand.

They didn't stop but continued on down the little valley. Joseph took a breath and felt safe for the moment, but he knew they would turn back before too long, and they would be watching for tracks, and watching the cover along the stream. He waited until they were well beyond him and then he got back on the horse and rode up the hill, once again to the east. He made it into the next valley, and then he turned northward.

He came to the road again before long, crossed it, and kept going north, urging the horse to stay at a trot for the present. But when he got well beyond the road, he got down and let the horse have some water and some rest. He had to believe the riders would not care enough to bother tracking him this far. As a little time passed, he began to feel safe. But now he had to push much farther north before he looped to the west. He decided not to go back to the road at all. There could well be other outposts closer to Far West.

Joseph moved on, but the slowness of the travel gradually brought back the rage he had felt all morning. At times he was tempted to gallop his horse again, to charge directly across the prairie into Far West. But he kept his head. He followed the valleys and he surveyed the land around him when he had to cross over hilltops. He had plenty of time to think, time to see the bodies in his mind—Sardius Smith and old Brother McBride. He wondered what kind of animals he was dealing with, what kind of men could commit such vile acts. He had thought he had seen men at their worst in Jackson County, but this was a deeper kind of evil.

As the sun was angling somewhat past its height, Joseph was heading southwest. He felt that he couldn't be more than a few miles from Far West. He was watching the horizon when he saw dark figures moving. He continued on, tentatively, and gradually he could see that it was a woman and a boy, and then he could see a little girl next to them, being pulled along. The woman was walking unsteadily, as though she were terribly tired.

Joseph guessed that she had to be a Mormon woman who had been driven from her home in some little settlement out on the prairie. Perhaps her husband had been killed. Joseph would have to help her whether he was delayed in getting to Far West or not.

He gave his horse a kick, hurrying it toward the woman. She didn't notice him at first, but when he approached her, she turned and faced him. She was holding a baby. Joseph could see the fear in her face. "Don't be afraid," Joseph yelled. "I've come to help you."

The woman stood and waited as Joseph got down from his horse. The little boy sat down, and the girl leaned against her mother. "Thank heaven," the woman said.

"Are you all right?" Joseph asked.

"Oh, yes. But I'm too tired to walk much fu'ther. I've come all the way from Daviess County today. My little ones is about to drop and so'm I."

"You can all get up on my horse and I'll lead you," Joseph said.

"If you could do that, I would be so thankful. It ain't much more than a mile now—maybe two."

"I'm afraid it's further than that, but we'll make it. Were you driven out, ma'am?"

"Oh, yes." She looked at Joseph, and he could see the panic still in her eyes. "Those devils came in and forced us out and then burned the house right to the ground. I didn't think such men existed in this world."

Joseph felt his rage again. He was impatient to get to the war. "Is your husband all right?" he asked.

"I s'pose. He's off with the militia. I hope he'll know where I've gone. I tried to tell those men that I wanted no trouble, but they just wouldn't listen. They had no mercy." Her voice was shaking as she relived it all.

"I know. I know how you feel. I've seen what they've done today. Maybe it's good your husband wasn't there. They might have killed him."

"I s'pose that's so." She took a breath, trying to keep her composure. "If you can just git me to my brother's house, south of here a little ways, I'll be all right for now."

"But your brother might have been driven out too. You would be better off to go to Far West. I think I can get you into town. You'll be safer there."

"Far West?"

"Yes, most of the outlying—"

"But thass the Mormon town."

"I know. It's . . ." And then Joseph realized. "But aren't you a Mormon?"

"A Mormon? Who do you think it was that burned us out?"

Joseph stared at the woman. She wasn't making any sense. She was wrong. The Saints wouldn't do that. And yet Joseph suddenly felt strange inside—nervous and empty, almost sick.

Time seemed to pass. Things changed. He saw the woman differently. She stepped back from him a little. "You can't be a Mormon," she said.

"Yes, ma'am." There was nothing to say now. They watched each other's eyes. Joseph could see her fear and confusion intensify.

"It couldn't have been Mormons," Joseph finally said. "You must be wrong about that."

"No," she said, nothing more. The boy, who was five or six, was looking up at Joseph. He was tired, his face blank. The woman sat down next to the boy in the brown and matted prairie grass. All was silent except that she seemed to be struggling to get her breath, and then she began to sob. She was a young woman, not more than twenty-five. She looked strong, almost muscular, but she was drained now. She had a scarf tied about her head, and she had wrapped a blanket about herself and about the baby. But her head was down now, her face toward the rotting prairie grass, and the sobs shook her whole body. The little girl was leaning against her mother still, but now she had crouched on her knees. Her eyes were shut and she seemed already asleep.

Joseph felt sorry for them—deeply sorry. But he did not believe her story. It couldn't possibly be true. He refused to accept it. And yet he was shaking, not just from exhaustion, not just from all he had been through that day, but also from a nameless fear—a powerful feeling that everything was wrong.

"Get on my horse," Joseph said. "I'll take you." But his words came out sounding almost angry.

She looked up. "Why?"

"Come on, hurry. I need to get to Far West. A mob attacked one of our towns last night. They killed off most of our men. They just killed them for no reason. I need to get help for those who are still alive." He wanted her to know. He wanted her to realize who the bad people were.

"But I thought only the Mormons was doing the mobbing and killing!"

"Who told you that?" Joseph said, and his voice was harsh with anger. "You've been told lies. People in Daviess County burned some of their own houses and blamed it on us. I know that for a fact."

"But it was Mormons that burned me out. They was Danites. They even said they was."

"No," Joseph said. "Get up now. Hurry. Get on my horse."

Joseph held the baby while the woman got up on the horse, straddling it and pulling her long skirt so that she could sit right. Then Joseph gave her the baby, who seemed to be asleep, and he helped the little girl up. She was only two or three and very little. She hardly weighed anything at all. She leaned down against the horse's neck and her eyes closed again. But Joseph was hurrying to put the little boy up behind his mother. "Where do we go?" he said.

"That way," the woman said, pointing. "It ain't far now."

"Can you find it? Do you know the way for sure?"

"Yes, it's close to where I used to live. I know these hills hereabouts."

Joseph set off walking, fast. He would get her there. He would prove to her what Mormons were. And he would not believe her. She was lying. Or at least she was mistaken. Someone was trying to make the Saints look bad by doing such things. But his insides were still quivering. He was thinking about Matthew, about Danites.

As it turned out, the house was even closer than the woman had thought. They crossed over the next hill, and then she spotted the road that led to the house, less than a mile away. Joseph walked hard and didn't say a word. The woman didn't speak either, but the baby had begun to cry. It was a plaintive cry, not healthy. After a minute or so, Joseph knew that the woman was nursing the baby. It had stopped crying abruptly, and Joseph could hear the gentle little grunts as it sucked. The sound seemed to grab at something deep in him. He clenched his teeth and tightened his hands into fists. He thought of little Samuel, and he thought of Sardius Smith. It was all too much—too much for one day. But he couldn't let go. He fought with all his strength to control himself.

Joseph helped the children down from the horse. The woman was trying to get the little girl to walk, and the boy was stumbling ahead on his own. Joseph thought he should say something more, but he didn't. He really didn't want to talk to her. He wanted to get away as fast as he could.

"Thank you," she said, turning back.

"That's all right."

"You ain't like those other men. They was all full of hate."

"But it wasn't us. Not Mormons. Do you understand that? I know it wasn't. We're just not like that. We could never do such . . ." But he stopped. He needed to get away from her.

She just looked at him, and then she shrugged. "I don't know. Maybe ever'body's like 'at sometimes."

"No!" he said, forcefully, but more to himself. He was riding now. "No. That's not true. There are people like that, but not everybody. Just animals, just wild men. Not Joseph Smith. Not Bishop Partridge. Not Father. Not Matthew." But he felt his throat tighten when he thought of Matthew. "Surely not Matthew." And then the pain seemed to grip his stomach— tight—the way it had the night before. He was afraid he was going to be sick again. But the passion was all gone—the hatred, the desire to hurt someone. He felt like crying. He wished that his father were still alive and that he could go home to him and be held in his strong arms.

But he had to fight back. He couldn't let himself cry. If he cried, it would mean that he believed the woman's story. But he would not believe her. Somehow she was wrong. She simply had to be wrong.

Joseph got into Far West by staying north, avoiding the army which he now could see camped to the south of town. Hundreds of men were out there on the prairie. But no battle had been fought—not yet. It was already late in the day when Joseph got into town. But he didn't go home. He went to the south part of town to where the Saints' militia had gathered.

Joseph looked for Hyrum Smith, but he couldn't find him. He did, however, find Brigham Young. He spilled out the information as quickly as he could, and Brother Brigham said he would send help if he could, but he hardly knew what could be done. A battle seemed to be coming. Joseph didn't stay to ask questions, however. He wanted to find Matthew.

The Saints had carried logs and wagons, fence rails, anything they could lay hands on, it seemed, and they had built a sort of barricade along the southern side of town. Joseph walked along it and kept asking for Matthew. There were fires all along the breastwork, and men seemed almost single file behind it. He finally found Matthew, leaning against an old wagon, his back to the army out on the prairie.

"Matthew, I need to talk to you. Can you come with me?"

"Where?"

"Just walk out a little. I need to ask you something."

"All right. Are you feeling sick?"

"No, I'm fine." But he did feel sick.

"What about Mother?"

"I haven't seen her since last night. I just got back from Haun's Mill. Brother Hyrum sent me."

"But Joseph, I told you to stay with—"

"The Brethren needed me to go, Matthew."

"All right. But go to Mother now." They were walking away

97

from the barricade, away from the other Mormon soldiers. Matthew's eyes looked tired and his face was red from the cold. Somehow he didn't look himself; he didn't look strong.

Joseph stopped and waited for Matthew to turn toward him. "What's going on, Matthew? I want you to tell me."

"There have been negotiations today, Joseph. We may end up fighting in the morning. I'm not sure."

"That's not what I mean. I want to know what the Danites are. I want to know why you came back from Diahman worried about your conscience."

Matthew's jaw tightened. "I can't tell you, Joseph."

"You've got to tell me, Matthew. I found a woman out on the prairie and she said that Mormons burned her house down. She said Danites did it. I know that's not true, but Matthew, I want you to tell me." Matthew looked into Joseph's face, but he didn't say anything. "Matthew, you have to tell me. I'm . . . scared. I don't understand what's . . . Listen, Matthew, at Haun's Mill they killed our people and hacked them up, even killed little boys. But that was *them,* Matthew. That was them. We're not like that."

"No, Joseph, we're *not* like that. You can trust that."

"Matthew, that's not enough. I can't just trust. You keep saying that to me, but I have to know for myself."

Matthew nodded. But he still didn't speak for a time. "All right, Joseph. I'll try to explain. But we have to move farther away. No one can hear this. And Joseph, you have to promise absolutely never to speak a word of this to anyone." The two of them moved farther back, away from the barricade, away from the Saints.

Chapter 13

The boys walked to a rail fence on the edge of town. Matthew leaned against it, half sitting on it, and Joseph stood in front of him. "Joseph, we're in a war," Matthew said. "We've been pushed and pushed, and our homes have been taken from us twice before—this time we're fighting back."

"I know that. But are we driving women and children out of their houses?"

Matthew wouldn't look at Joseph. "Maybe that *has* happened, Joseph. I don't know for sure. Some of our people have become so angry—and so tired of what we've put up with—that they think we should give the old settlers some of their own medicine."

"But it's not right, Matthew."

"No. It isn't right." Matthew was looking down at the ground.

"Matthew, why didn't you want to go to Crooked River?"

"Joseph, it's not easy to explain." He seemed to be searching for the right words. "See, I don't blame people for fighting back. It's about time we did. But I think . . . Well, I don't know. It just seems to me that it got out of hand up in Daviess County."

"What do you mean, Matthew?" Joseph stepped a little to his left. He wanted to see Matthew's face better.

But Matthew didn't speak for some time, and he still wouldn't look up. "We ended up splitting up into four groups up there. General Parks told us to defend ourselves, and so we went out to stop the old settlers at their games. They were burning houses and killing off our cattle—trampling our cornfields. All the things we've seen before. One of our companies went over to Gallatin, and from what I could find out, they burned down the store and some of the houses. But before they burned the store, they carried all the goods in the store and brought them back to Diahman—they said it was consecrated goods, to save the Saints."

"Why did they do it, Matthew?"

"Well, Joseph, we were being starved out, almost the same as in DeWitt. And all the Saints who lived in the outlying settlements were being forced into town, where there just wasn't enough food. So they retaliated. It was a way of striking back, of saying to the old settlers that they couldn't keep pushing us without some resistance."

"But Matthew . . ." Joseph didn't know what to say.

Matthew looked up at him squarely. "It just got carried away, Joseph. Men in my company were stealing cattle and chickens, anything they could get their hands on. And in a way I don't blame them. It was war. But Joseph, they were so . . . I don't know. They *enjoyed* it. They were laughing about it. They called the stolen cattle buffalo and the hogs wild boar. It was as though the stealing made them happy. I guess it did feel good in a way, after all they had been through."

Joseph was thinking. He was trying to sort it all out—accept what he was hearing. "I stole a boat," he said.

"I know you did. And you were justified. Right now we're

doing things we wouldn't normally do. But I don't want you to think we've turned bad, Joseph."

"What are the Danites?"

Matthew glanced around, apparently checking to see that no one was near. "Joseph, can you settle for what I've told you?"

"I don't think so. I saw that woman, Matthew. She had been burned out of her house with her little children. She said the men were crazy—like devils. And she said they were Danites."

Matthew stared ahead, toward the barricade, toward the enemy out on the field. "I took a vow, Joseph. I said I would never reveal *anything* about the Danites. It could even be dangerous for me to break that vow."

"Dangerous? You mean they would punish you? What kind of people are they?"

"They're not bad people, Joseph. Not really. I'm one of them."

"What?"

"You heard me."

"Matthew, now you have to tell me. Things aren't making much sense to me right now."

"Joseph, we've hardly done anything back to the old settlers—not compared to what they've done to us."

"Matthew, that isn't really the point, and you know it!" Joseph's voice had risen, but silence followed. More quietly, he finally said, "If we have some group going around burning people's houses—and you're one of them—then we're no better than they are."

"But it's not quite like you think."

"All right. Tell me. But Matthew, do you remember how we felt about *them* when they made us leave *our* house?"

"Yes. Of course I remember." He stood up straight and stepped a little closer to Joseph. "I'll tell you some things, all

101

right? But you must never say anything to anyone. You have to vow to me that you won't."

"I do. I promise."

"All right." Matthew spoke softly. "First of all, the group was formed earlier this last summer. When they asked me to join, they said it was a defense company—to protect the Saints. We were separate from the militia, but we were a special group that was to be ready for any difficulties that would come up. I was all for it at the time. But it's changed, Joseph. The man in charge of it has—"

"Who, Matthew?"

"I don't think I should say."

"But you have to. It isn't one of the Brethren is it, not one of our leaders?"

"No, Joseph—it's Brother Avard. But I don't know what has happened. The man has gotten carried away. He's preaching all kinds of crazy things now. He says you can do anything—kill, steal, anything—and if it's in the name of the Lord, and for his kingdom, it's not wrong. It's people who believe that who are now doing things like—well, like burning that woman's house."

"Matthew, all these years, since we came out here, it's always been the old settlers. They were the bad ones. But now it's us too."

"No, Joseph. Most of the Saints would never act that way. A lot more of the old settlers have done those things."

Joseph stood and thought. The numbers didn't seem to matter very much at the moment. Things had always been simple before today. The bad people had always been on the other side.

"Joseph, it's just been a few. Even most of the Danites don't approve of what Avard has been saying. They just don't dare argue with him."

"Does Joseph Smith know?" That was the crucial question for Joseph, the one that scared him most.

"No. I don't think so. He knew that we formed the group, but I don't think he has any idea what Avard is preaching lately."

"Why didn't you go to the Prophet and tell him?"

"I've thought about it. Maybe I will yet. But we vowed absolute silence. Joseph, I could be killed for what I've told you."

"Killed?"

"Yes, killed. Avard has vowed to destroy anyone who breaks the vow—and leave his body to the buzzards."

Joseph felt sick again. It was all so evil—so secret and wrong. He couldn't think of anything more to say. All morning he had wanted to hurt someone, and now he wanted to run somewhere and hide.

"You'd better get home now, Joseph. Go home and rest. I'll talk to you again when we have more time. But don't turn against the Saints—not because of Avard and those few who have gotten all mixed up. Think of Bishop Partridge. Think of Parley Pratt. Think of the Prophet. We're not bad, Joseph—we're not!"

Joseph nodded, but he couldn't talk. Matthew touched his shoulder, and when he did, it opened up the emotions that Joseph had been feeling since he had met the woman. He had to hurry away so that Matthew wouldn't see him. He was relieved to get away from the barricade. He had wanted to fight; he had wanted to be a man. But now he wanted to be with his mother. He wished that he could talk to her about everything, but he knew he couldn't. At least he could be with someone he knew was good. More than anything, Joseph wished that Father were alive. He wanted so much to talk to him.

* * *

Joseph went home. He didn't tell his mother or the others what he had seen at Haun's Mill, nor about the woman on the prairie. He told them that he would talk later, but that he needed

103

to eat and sleep now. But he didn't sleep, not at all. He was tired beyond belief, but he lay still and listened to his mind rehearse it all over again, especially the conversation with Matthew. He didn't blame Matthew for joining the Danites, and he respected him for his conscience. He could even understand that some of the Saints would go too far, not control their desire for revenge. And yet he was not satisfied. He was in a new world, suddenly, where evil was much closer than he had ever imagined. And he was angry about it. He hated to see things become so confused. He had wanted the woman to be wrong. But now her story was undeniable, and Joseph felt changed, as though he had left himself out on the prairie.

It was still not late. Only the little children were in bed, but the house was quiet, even tense. Joseph lay listening to the sound of his own breathing, and to the popping of the fire down below. Then he heard a sound, shrill and distant at first, and unidentifiable. It gradually became wild and powerful, like the howling of thousands of animals. He jumped up. He heard Mother say, "They're coming." Joseph had never undressed, and now he was down the ladder in seconds. The sound continued, a wild, high-pitched scream that was not one sound but hundreds blended together.

He stood listening, trying to find in his memory some comparable noise. Sister Engbert was on her feet, with her head cocked, listening intently. Ruth and the Engbert girls looked stunned.

The sound continued, even intensified, and the guns were sounding now—in the distance. Joseph didn't know what to do.

Chapter 14

The noise continued, rolling in waves, subsiding at times, and then coming back all the more forcefully. "It's men screaming," Mother said.

Joseph nodded. He knew she was right. He could hear the yelps amid the one steady roar. "I don't think they're attacking," Joseph said. "The sound is staying out on the prairie."

"Then why are they doing it?" Sister Engbert said, and her voice was full of the tenseness that was in the room. "Are they going to attack now—when it's getting dark?"

"I don't think so," Joseph said, but he wasn't sure why. There was something in the sound that didn't seem like a battle cry. And then he knew what it was. "They sound too happy," he said. "It sounds like a victory cry. Maybe we've surrendered."

Joseph went to the fire and sat down. Sister Williams sat down close by, and Ruth came and sat on her lap. The sound went on and on. It became increasingly apparent, however, that it was not coming closer. No one talked, and everyone listened. After a time Joseph felt as though he couldn't stand to sit there any longer. He wanted to find out what was happening. He worried, however, about leaving his mother and the rest.

Finally Mary Ann got up and walked across the room. It was not easy for her to sit still very long. "Why do they keep doing that?" she said to no one in particular.

"Never mind," Sister Engbert said. "Just sit down and don't get yourself all worked up."

But she didn't sit down. "I'll bet Joseph is right," she said. "I'll bet we've given up again without even a fight. I wish I were out there with a gun."

Joseph's head popped around. He stared at her. "Well, what's the matter with you?" she said. "You sit here by the fire where you're safe, when you ought to be out there with the men, seeing to it that—"

"Mary Ann!" Sister Engbert said. "You hush immediately. You have no right to say such things."

"Well, it's true. He isn't even a good messenger boy. He comes back from a battle so scared he can't even talk."

Joseph was irritated but he wasn't angry. She had no idea. She was a child, and this was all a game to her. Joseph stood up calmly. "Mother," he said, "I'm going to walk to the barricade and see what's going on. I won't be long."

"Joseph, don't let her upset you. We need you here."

Joseph glanced at Mary Ann. She was not smiling, not triumphant. He sensed that she was sorry, that she wished she could take some of her words back.

"I won't be long, Mother. It'll help us all to know exactly what is happening. They seem to be quieting down out there now."

Mother said nothing more, and Joseph got his coat and walked out. It was an old coat, a shabby one that was too small for him, and he was still wearing the old, oversized boots that Joseph Smith had given him in DeWitt. But DeWitt seemed years in the past now.

He found Matthew where he had been before, but now Matthew, like most of the soldiers, was standing up, peering over the barricade at the other camp. Joseph could see the fires, and he could see movement, just shadows before the flames. The movement seemed almost like a dance, the shadows gyrating more or less rhythmically. And there were still yelps and screams, if not the steady roar. It was baffling to Joseph. He had never seen humans behave this way. He was trying to relate it to anything that he understood.

"What are they doing, Matthew?"

Matthew turned around. "You shouldn't be here," he said, and Joseph could see that he was changed from what he had been a couple of hours before. He looked tired and hopeless, and his face was harsh.

"Everyone was frightened, Matthew. We need to know what's going on out there."

"They took the Prophet. That's what they're celebrating about."

"What do you mean, they took him?"

"Well," Matthew said, but he hesitated, as though the telling of the story would take more energy than he possessed right then. "Colonel Hinkle talked to General Lucas this afternoon and—"

"You mean Lucas from Jackson County? The one who helped drive us out?"

"That's right, Joseph. That's who's leading that so-called army out there. I guess he told Brother Hinkle that he would discuss a treaty with Joseph Smith and some of the leaders. At least that's what Brother Hinkle claimed. But when Joseph Smith rode out there—with Sidney Rigdon, Lyman Wight, Parley Pratt, and George Robinson—Lucas's men just surrounded them and took them back into camp. That's when all the howling started."

"But how could a man call himself a general and do something like that?"

"I don't know, Joseph. Some people around here think it was Hinkle who betrayed the Prophet and agreed to deliver him into their hands."

Joseph wondered which side of the barricade the enemy was on. He really didn't need any more of this, not right now. He needed to know the enemy, even if it were just so he could know whom to fear.

Matthew turned back around, and the two of them stared at the distant fires and the feathery shadows around them. "Didn't they get Brother Hyrum?" Joseph asked.

"No, he didn't go out there. Someone said that he's home in bed, sick."

"Who will lead us now?"

"I don't know, Joseph. Maybe there's nothing to lead. Maybe we're finished."

It was turning cold again, and a fine mist was beginning to fall. Rain would be coming again or maybe snow. Joseph watched his breath puff out before him. He tried to think what would happen to them now, but he couldn't even decide what to expect the next morning. Would they attack now—try to destroy the Saints? Or were they satisfied? Maybe they would kill Brother Joseph and the others; maybe they already had. In fact, that might have been the reason for their joy.

Matthew was a little in front of Joseph, but facing out toward the prairie. "They're worse than we are, Joseph," he said.

Joseph stood and looked into the fires. He was still numb from the day he had put in, but some of the anger was returning. "Are they?" he asked.

"A hundred times worse. We can't even begin to compete with evil like that. Look at them. You should have seen them before the sun went down. Gilliam's men are there now, the ones from up in Daviess County. They were dressed up in war paint, like Indians. We could see them dancing around the fires and acting like wild men. I think they're possessed, Joseph."

Joseph wanted to take solace in that evil, wanted to agree with Matthew. But he was still not used to the idea that *any* human beings could act that way.

He went back home. He told Mother what she needed to know, and then he went to bed. And finally he slept, but he dreamed about his horse again, about the warmth of summer and the sky, and sometimes he saw wild animals flopping about before a red-orange fire. Toward morning, while it was still dark, he gradually realized he was awake and where he was. Samuel had nestled close to him. He had found Joseph in the dark and huddled next to him. Joseph held him close and waited for the sun to come up, wondering what the day would bring. Samuel was warm and so very little. He seemed totally relaxed and secure. Joseph thought of the boy who had been sleeping at Haun's Mill, but he quickly forced the image away. He wanted to remember the sound the little baby had made—the one nursing as Joseph had led the horse. Rain was falling now, the drops pattering on the roof just above Joseph. The sound was peaceful, something normal for a change. Joseph wanted never to move— just to stay where he was.

A while later, as the sun was first rising, Joseph heard his mother say, "Oh, no." Horses were coming, riding hard. Someone outside yelled, not far from the house. And then there were whoops, not like the night before, not full of joy, but excited and intense. Joseph slipped away from Samuel, and then covered him with the blankets again. He got up, dressed quickly, and hurried down the ladder. Just as he reached the floor, he heard gunfire. His mother was sitting up in bed, and the Engbert girls, all on the floor, were also sitting up.

Joseph looked out the window and saw two riders go by in the half-light of first dawn. They were yelping and waving their pistols. "They're shooting in the air," Joseph said. "They just want to scare us."

"How did they get into town?" Mother asked, her voice anxious.

"We must have surrendered. They must have taken over the town."

For almost an hour riders passed back and forth through Far West, continuing to yelp and to terrorize the people. Ruth was beside herself, crying and pleading with her mother and with Joseph to reassure her. And when someone was heard at the door, Ruth panicked and began to scream, but it was Matthew who spoke from outside. When he came in, Joseph knew the Saints were defeated. Matthew had never looked so broken.

"Is it over?" Mother asked.

Matthew looked at Mother and then at Ruth, who was still clinging to her mother's dress. "Yes, it's over."

"What now, Matthew?"

"Governor Boggs issued an order. We have to give up our weapons and promise to leave the state. Either that or be exterminated."

"Exterminated?"

"That was the word he used."

"Why didn't you fight?" Mary Ann said, and her voice was full of hostility.

"Hush, Mary Ann," Sister Engbert said.

Matthew glanced her way, seemed to take little note of her, and then looked back at his mother. "There are thousands of them out there now. We wouldn't stand a chance. And now that they have our leaders, we . . . we just couldn't."

"Where will we go?" Joseph asked.

Joseph didn't like to hear Matthew talk that way. He looked so stooped, the way Father had looked after the beating, after he had tried to get better and couldn't.

Mother could see it too. "We'll be all right," she said. "We can start over again."

Matthew walked to the fire and sat down. He leaned over and put his elbows on his knees and then held his head in his hands, the palms against his temples. "That's right," he said. "We'll be fine. We can build again." But his voice was empty.

Joseph was hanging on, and he knew Matthew was too. But if Matthew broke down, if he began to cry, Joseph feared they would all be finished. And Matthew was not far from tears. But Ruth was the only one who cried, and the rest of the family tried to comfort her. At least they were still alive, they told her. But Ruth kept saying, "Not again. Do we have to leave again?"

Mother took Ruth in her arms and held her while she sobbed. And then Matthew got up. "We won't have to leave until spring—or at least that's what we've been hearing. We'll not have an easy winter. Joseph, we need to go get all the corn we can out of the crib, before it's all stolen by this mob."

"How can we do that with all of them riding around the town?"

"We'll manage. We'll figure something out."

Joseph took a deep breath and felt some life coming back. He knew that Matthew *would* manage, that he *would* figure something out.

Chapter 15

Joseph, Matthew, and Brother Engbert, along with the Engbert girls, walked back and forth all that day carrying baskets of corn. The horses had been stolen, and so had the mules. There was simply no other way to get the corn into town. Some of the enemy soldiers threatened and cursed them, but no one stopped them from making the mile-long walk over and over again. In the afternoon Mary Ann made the trip with Joseph a couple of times. She looked tired, and she was subdued. She had never apologized to Joseph, or to Matthew, for the things she had said, but her hostility was clearly gone.

The next day, in the morning, Matthew was called to the square and told to bring his weapons. But this was not a call to arms, and everyone knew it. It was an official surrender, a time for giving up weapons. Joseph also walked to the square, just to see what was happening. The Mormon troops were formed into two companies and then marched out of town onto the prairie. Joseph followed along behind. The band that had played so triumphantly on the Fourth of July was now playing a plaintive song that someone said was Washington's death march. On the prairie the old settlers' militias had formed a huge open square, and the smaller Mormon force was marched into it. The Mormons were called to attention, forming a square of their own, with their backs to the old settlers and facing the center. Then, one by one, the Mormon men marched to the middle of the square and placed their weapons on the growing heap. Some stabbed their swords into the ground and then broke the blades. Joseph could see the frustration, the humiliation, on the men's somber faces. The mockery never stopped, the old settlers calling out insults incessantly, and it was surely all the Mormon men could do to withstand the temptation to return it. Joseph felt the old anger again, along with fear and the sense of gloom that hung over everything now. It was difficult to sort out such emotions.

After the guns—many of them just squirrel rifles or old muskets—were turned over, the Mormon soldiers were marched to a table at the center of the formation. Here the men were forced to sign a document that gave away the deeds to their properties in the county. This was supposed to pay for the expenses of the "war." The process was slow. Many of the Mormons sat down on the ground as they waited, but the old settlers' troops, most of them on horseback, gradually grew restless, and some of them began to ride into town. When Joseph saw this, he decided he had better head for home.

In town men were riding about, screaming and shooting their guns. Few Mormons were outside. Some of the old settlers had collected near the town square and were passing around jugs of whiskey. Joseph got past them as quickly as he could and headed down the street toward his house. But two men rode down the road on horseback and came up behind him. Joseph moved far to the side of the road and kept walking.

"Whar yuh goin' to, boy?" one of them said. "Won't Joe Smith let you carry a gun?"

Joseph kept walking. When he reached his cabin he turned in, but the men reined up their horses just as Joseph was passing through the dooryard. "Hey, boy, have you got a chicken or two around yer place? We're gittin' tired of salt pork and johnny cake."

Joseph went in and latched the door. His mother came to him. "Who's out there?"

"Just some men."

"What do they want?"

"They said they want some chickens." Just then someone knocked on the door. Joseph hesitated, and his mother stepped back. Joseph could hear the Engbert girls moving to the back of the room. Joseph didn't want to open the door, but he feared what the men might do if he didn't. The knock came again, hard this time, shaking the door. Joseph opened it.

A hand came through the opening, grabbing Joseph's coat. "Listen, boy, when I talk to you, you answer. Un'erstand?"

Joseph was pulled toward the man. He was not big, but he had a flat, ugly face and a big head. He smelled of whiskey. Joseph didn't answer, hardly had a chance to.

"Do you un'erstand that, boy?" He shook Joseph, suddenly and violently.

"Yes," Joseph said, and he was frightened.

"Aw right." The man pushed Joseph back and stepped into the house. The other man came in behind him. "Well, now, ain't this a fine covey of little women in here?"

The second man, taller and red-faced with big ears and long side-whiskers, stared at the girls, who were close together in the far corner. "Shore ugly though, ain't they?" he said.

"I dunno. That little one there—the one in the middle—she ain't so bad. I'll bet she'd like you, Harvey. Why don't you give 'er a little kiss an' see if she don't like it?"

Joseph took a step to his right, in front of the second man, the taller one. "No," he said. That was all.

The man began to laugh. And then, without warning, he grabbed Joseph and thrust him across the room. "He's got some grit, that boy," he said. He made no move toward Mary Ann.

Joseph had been thrown to his knees. He got up and walked back, standing in front of the man again.

But Mother said, "Never mind, Joseph." She turned to the man who had come in first. "What do you want?" There was authority in her voice.

"Say, Harvey," the man said, grinning, "this is the one I like. She ain't no spring chicken, but she's not a bad looker. I'll bet she'd like to have herself a real man after being married to one of these Mormon preachers."

"Leave my house," Sister Williams said. "Now."

Both men laughed. Joseph stepped up closer to his mother. He didn't know what he could do, and it was frustrating, but he knew it was his place to be there, to do something. "They both got a little grit in 'em." The shorter man grinned at Sister Williams. "Now listen, little lady. We ain't about to harm you or yer tender girls over there. What would you take us for? What we want is some decent food. We been sleepin' out there in that miserable ol' leaky tent, eatin' nothin' but corn pone and cold pork. It was a bad night last night too. Rained all night. I shore felt sorry for Joe Smith and them others that had to sleep on the ground." This brought another hacking laugh. "But then it don't matter too much if he ketched himself a fever. We're goin' to put him out of his misery anyhow—in fact, by now he might be all taken care of."

The men were grinning again when Sister Williams asked, "Are you really going to shoot him?" She had used a surprising

115

tone, not hostile, almost as though she were asking a friend. The men stopped laughing.

"Well, I don't know, ma'am. That's what everyone says."

"But why?"

"Well, ma'am, that's not for people like you and me to talk about." But he was clearly uncomfortable. "We jist wondered if you had some fresh meat."

"There are chickens out back, in the coop. I'm sure you know that. But we have a long winter ahead, and not much to survive on. I suppose you're going home to better food soon."

"Well, I'm not zactly shore." The taller man stepped back toward the door, as though he wanted out. Joseph couldn't believe what he was seeing.

"Well, you take what you want," Mother said. "I have no way to stop you. But when you get home I want you to tell your wives and children what heroes you've been."

The tall man stepped out the door. "Come on," he said. They walked out to their horses, got on, and rode away. Mother shut the door.

"How did you do that?" Joseph asked.

"They're humans, Joseph. They get out there around those fires screaming and acting crazy and they forget it, but they remember fast when someone reminds them."

Joseph felt terribly young, and he knew that he had under-estimated his mother's understanding of things.

* * *

Matthew came back in the afternoon and said that Hyrum Smith and some of the other brethren had now been taken into custody. But it was the next afternoon when Matthew came into the house and said, "Why don't you all come to the town square? They're taking Joseph Smith away—and some of the others—

116

but they've brought them into town. I guess they're going to let them say good-bye to their families—I'm not sure. But folks are gathering at the square."

Joseph hurried out; he didn't wait for the others. He ran toward the square. There was a big crowd, both Mormons and old settlers, standing in the rain. Joseph could see two covered wagons in the center. But then he saw the crowd open, and a cluster of soldiers was coming through, pushing someone along. It was the Prophet. Joseph was close to the Prophet's house, and so he stayed there, knowing the soldiers were bringing him home.

In a few seconds the crowd bulged backward and pushed toward him. Joseph moved close to Joseph Smith's front fence and waited. The soldiers were pushing him hard, hurrying him along. He looked tired and disheveled, his matted hair falling forward in his face. One side of his face was streaked with dirt and his clothes were muddy all over and soaking wet. As they pushed him through his front gate, there was a little struggle. "Could I go in alone?" the Prophet asked.

"No." They forced him ahead. Two of the soldiers went inside and the others waited in the dooryard. The door was left open and Joseph could see the soldiers inside, but not the Prophet. He was not gone long, however. After only a few minutes he was being pushed out the door again. He had a rolled blanket in his arms. Emma came out behind him. The Prophet struggled to turn and look at her. And then little Joseph, the Prophet's young son, slipped by the soldiers and grabbed his father's legs.

One of the soldiers cursed the boy and then grabbed him and pulled him loose.

"Don't hurt him," Joseph Smith said, but the man turned the boy around, roughly, and shoved him back toward the house.

"Don't worry, Emma," the Prophet said, trying to twist his head to see her again. "I'll be all right."

One of the soldiers cursed the Prophet and then shoved him from behind. The soldier turned around and looked at Emma. "Don't ever plan to see this man again," he said. "He'll be shot for his crimes."

Emma put her hands to her face and a sister hurried to her. Then the Prophet was gone, back through the crowd. Joseph had wanted to touch him, or at least wish him well, but he hadn't been able to get close enough.

There had been a crowd down the street at Hyrum Smith's home too. Not only had Hyrum been sick, but so had his wife, and she was expecting a baby soon.

Joseph ran toward the crowd at the square and then he worked his way through it. He wanted to get to the wagon, have one last look at the Brethren. He feared they would never return. But the crowd was straining forward, and Joseph made slow progress. An old settler pushed Joseph when he tried to squeeze past him, and so Joseph worked his way to his left and then slipped ahead. It took him several minutes, but he got to the front, or at least close enough to it to see the wagons. Joseph Smith, however, had already been put inside, and so had Hyrum. Sidney Rigdon was being pushed into the back of one of the wagons now. He was not as young as the others, not as robust. He looked pale and frightened, defeated.

In another few minutes Parley Pratt was brought through the crowd. Joseph remembered the peaceful days when Brother Pratt had been his schoolteacher in the old Colesville settlement in Jackson County. He was a firm man, broad-faced and bulldoggish in appearance, but he was gentle and full of goodness. Now he was being treated like an animal. Joseph knew that Parley's wife was ill. She was a frail woman who wouldn't handle this well.

Someone said that Lyman Wight and George Robinson were also in one of the other wagons, and Amasa Lyman was soon brought through the crowd and added to the number. When Joseph saw the people parting again, he wondered which of the other brethren was being taken, but in time he could see that it was Lucy Smith, the Prophet's mother, and her teenaged daughter, also named Lucy. The two were guided to the wagon by a soldier, but Joseph and Hyrum were not allowed to get out. "You say what you have to say," one of the guards told Sister Smith. "They can hear you. We aren't pulling them out again."

Sister Smith stood near the front of the wagon. She said something, speaking through the wagon's cover. Joseph couldn't hear her, but in a moment he saw a hand slip out from under the loosely tacked canvas. Sister Smith took hold of the hand, grasping it in both of hers. She was still speaking through the cover. Young Lucy also took the hand, and Joseph could see her body tremble as she sobbed. The people had become quiet now. Joseph saw a woman nearby crying, tears running down her face. And the rain was still falling, making a gentle rustling sound, soaking the men's hats and women's white caps. The gloom and the cold mixed with the anguish and the frustration. It was the lowest moment the Saints had ever lived through—Joseph understood that. And it was a terrible moment for Joseph. When his father had died he had at least felt pain; now he felt cold and numb and vanquished.

Sister Smith and Lucy stepped toward the back of the wagon and once again a hand slipped out. They each held the hand for a time, and then, just as the guards were demanding they move back, young Lucy bent and kissed it. Lucy was forced back, and the wagon rolled away, pushing through the crowd. The people were amazingly silent. They simply stood and watched as the wagons slowly moved away. More people were crying than not, but no one spoke until the wagons were out of sight.

Chapter 16

The weekend passed with no church meetings allowed and with soldiers everywhere. The Saints had lost a war without fighting, and they were now occupied by the enemy. Militia men came back to the Williams' house and took all their chickens and even their cow. Cattle were being shot down throughout Far West and on the farms outside town. The cornfields were trampled by the old settlers' hundreds of horses, and corn in the cribs was carried off for fodder. Fortunately, Matthew and Joseph had brought home their pork on the day they had carried in the corn. This gave the Williamses and Engberts more to live on than many families had.

In the next few days new stories spread through town. Emma Smith had been forced out of her house while the place was ransacked and everything of value was carried off. Earlier Brother Carey had been struck over the head with a rifle butt and had died from loss of blood. And though Joseph wasn't told about it until later, some of the Mormon women were raped.

On Monday General Clark called the Saints to the town square. He was the general who had actually been commissioned to handle the "Mormon War" by Governor Boggs, but he had arrived with a large army only after General Lucas had taken affairs into his own hands. And it was Lucas who had taken Joseph Smith and the other brethren off to be paraded through the streets of Independence. Only later did the Saints learn that Lucas had ordered Joseph Smith shot on the second night of his captivity. But Alexander Doniphan, an officer in the militia himself, had refused to carry out the order, calling it cold-blooded murder.

General Clark took his place atop a wagon and spoke to the crowd of Saints and militia men. He read off a long list of names, all of men who were leaders in the Church in the various settlements. These men were called out and then marched off, fifty-six of them. He said they would be taken to jail and tried for their crimes. And then he delivered a speech that all the Saints would remember with bitterness for years to come. He told them they had complied with the first provisions of the treaty by giving up their leaders, their weapons, and their property. Now they had to leave the state.

He was being lenient, he said; he was allowing them to stay for the winter. But if they put in crops in the spring, or showed any intent to stay on, he would not be so merciful again. "You need not expect mercy," he said, "but extermination, for I am determined the governor's order shall be executed." Joseph shivered. He remembered Sidney Rigdon's words on the Fourth of July. It had been Brother Rigdon who had first suggested the idea of extermination—and now the words were coming back to haunt the Saints. "As for your leaders" Clark continued, "do not once think—do not for a moment—do not let it enter your mind, that they will be delivered or that you will see their faces again, for their fate is fixed—their die is cast—their doom is sealed."

Joseph felt the sense of gloom spread over him again. The

thought of losing the Prophet was almost more than he could stand. He refused to believe it could happen.

General Clark said he was dismayed that such intelligent people could be caught up in the chains of superstition and fanaticism. He told the Saints to scatter and never organize into a body again. "You have always been the aggressors—you have brought upon yourselves these difficulties by being disaffected and not being subject to rule—and my advice is that you become as other citizens, lest by a recurrence of these events you bring upon yourselves irretrievable ruin."

That was it. The Saints took the bitter medicine without reply. But there was weeping as they returned to their homes. The men from over sixty families had been taken away. No one knew whether any would ever be freed. And beyond that was the taste of bitterness, the appalling accusation of being the aggressors—after all the Saints had been through, especially in the last few days.

Joseph had not seen Emma Smith in the crowd, but he saw Lydia Partridge, with two of her daughters. They were walking back across the road to their home. Sister Partridge was standing straight, and yet, when Joseph caught a glimpse of her face, he could see the pain. Emily and Eliza were crying, but Sister Partridge was not. Joseph could see that she was steeling herself, readying herself for the worst.

Mary Ann was with Joseph, and the two walked back to the house together. Mary Ann was livid. "Joseph, how can he have the nerve to stand up there and say we started it all?"

"I don't know, Mary Ann. They see the whole thing from the other side."

"What other side?"

"They think we're trying to take over."

"But we've never hurt anyone." Joseph didn't respond; he

had no desire to say more. "We didn't even fight, Joseph. We just gave up."

Joseph let his breath out in a little puff that quickly floated away in the rather stiff breeze. "Sometimes we fought, Mary Ann. You don't know everything. We fought in Gallatin."

"You mean at the election? That was nothing. We only—"

"No, not at the election. We burned the store and some of the houses."

"*We* did?"

Joseph nodded, and that was all he was going to say. Mary Ann took a few steps without saying anything, and then she said, "Good." When Joseph turned to look at her, she said, "Well, I'm glad to hear we got a little revenge. Aren't you?"

"I don't know, Mary Ann."

"You would have fought if you had to, Joseph. You were ready to fight for me."

Joseph's face suddenly felt hot. He refused to look at Mary Ann. Now he understood why she had been so nice to him lately. But Joseph also realized that he *had* been ready to fight for her. He had not thought of it that way before. "Mother's way was better," he finally said.

"But it doesn't always work, Joseph. Sometimes you have to fight." Joseph glanced at Mary Ann, and she was taking a quick look at him at the same time. Then she looked forward again, but she was smiling just a bit. "But you don't have to think you're a hero," she said.

Joseph tried not to smile, but he couldn't quite hold back.

* * *

In a few days the Saints at Adam-ondi-Ahman were driven from their homes and forced to come to Far West. Many of them had to camp out for the winter in their wagons and tents. There were simply not enough log houses in Far West to accommodate all the people who had been forced to come there. The Williamses took in another family, Brother Jenson and his wife and two little girls. And so there were seventeen in the one-room cabin. At least there were two men to help chop wood and haul it in, and there were two women to help Sister Williams grate the boiled corn. It was a never-ending job, but corn was almost the only food available, except for the slowly rationed pork and potatoes, and the few pumpkins that had been saved.

It was a harsh winter, and the suffering of the Saints was terrible. Gradually, some of them decided not to wait until spring, since they were exposed to the weather anyway. They began to pull out, a few at a time, and traverse the state to Illinois or to eastern Iowa. Most of the Saints gathered around Quincy, Illinois, but no official gathering place had been established.

Most of the men who had been taken to the jail in Richmond were eventually released after six weeks of living in disgusting conditions. A mock trial—what was supposed to be a hearing—took place in Richmond for Joseph Smith and some of the other leaders. But when witnesses for the defense were listed by the leaders, the men on the list were immediately added to those in jail. It became a hopeless cause, and Alexander Doniphan, now the attorney for the defense, suggested they concede and hope for someone other than Judge King at the trial. And so Joseph Smith and Hyrum, along with Sidney Rigdon, Lyman Wight, Caleb Baldwin, and Alexander McRae, were taken to a jail in Liberty, Missouri. Parley Pratt and a few others continued to be held in Richmond.

Brigham Young, along with Heber Kimball, gradually took over the direction of the exodus from Missouri. Most of the leaders who had been jailed had been forced to flee the state, because of threats against their lives, but Brigham Young and Heber

Kimball were not so well known among the old settlers since they had both been on missions during much of the time the Saints had been in Far West. Brigham Young was tireless in organizing, in helping to see that the poor had means, in finding wagons for those who were without. The Saints who were better off were encouraged to give to the poor, that all might leave the state by spring.

It was a tedious winter with far too little to do and little to look forward to. Matthew tried to speak well of Illinois. He told Joseph he had learned plenty, and that this time he would make fewer mistakes in rebuilding. But Joseph didn't think his heart was much in it, and he often caught Matthew staring into the fire, looking lost. The two of them wandered out to the farm sometimes, but only for a walk. Now there were no plans and no point in keeping things up. The wagon was the only thing worth caring for, and they didn't even have a team to pull it. The only meaningful job anymore was chopping wood to keep the crowded house warm for the children.

Mother's life was mostly taken up with keeping the large group fed, but Joseph was impressed with her resolution, her will to survive. Samuel fell sick again in December. He would seem to come out of it a bit, but then would relapse into coughing spells. Sometimes it was hard for him to breathe, and Matthew and Joseph would trade off with Mother, sitting by him all night, making sure that he didn't choke or smother. Mother knew that he was dangerously close to pneumonia, and she was constantly worried.

Ruth and the younger Engbert girl tried to make the best of things. They talked and went for walks and even played with Ruth's rag doll. Ruth was no longer so frightened. She knew they had to leave again, and this was not easy for her, but at least the dread was over. It was now a simple reality.

One day early in January, Joseph and Matthew were in the woods chopping fallen trees. Brother Engbert and Brother Jenson had borrowed a team, and they were loading and hauling what the boys had chopped. It was a sunny day, and somewhat warmer than it had been for a time. Matthew worked hard, and Joseph tried to keep up with him. Sometime toward noon they finally sat down on a big log to take a rest.

"Matthew," Joseph said, "if we can get land again—and we can start over—you'll stay with us, won't you?"

"Stay with you? What do you mean? Where would I be going?"

"I don't know. But you'll be nineteen soon. Maybe you'll want to get married and move off."

"I'm not about to do that, Joseph, and you know it."

"But you'll get married sometime."

"I won't leave you, Joseph, not until you're ready to handle things."

"Could I handle things now?"

"Well, I suppose you could if you had to. But there's no reason for it. Not yet."

Joseph stretched his back, which was aching from the steady chopping all morning. He had known what Matthew would say, but he had wanted reassurance. Few things frightened him so much as the idea of losing Matthew. "What about Emily Cox?" Joseph said, and he couldn't help but smile a little.

"I don't think I ever heard that name before," Matthew said, and he smiled too, if only slightly.

"Don't you really like her anymore?" Joseph said, more seriously.

Matthew seemed unready to say anything. He looked at Joseph and his smile had faded. "Well, Joseph, I never did get all that—"

"Come on, Matthew," Joseph said, laughing now. "Tell the truth."

Matthew looked annoyed. "All right. Here's the truth. Mother was right about her. The last I heard, her family left the Church and went to live in Liberty—just when all the trouble started. I understand now that she's engaged to some old settler's son."

"Is your heart broken?"

Matthew reached out and pushed Joseph, knocking him off the log backward. But Joseph only lay on his back and laughed. It felt so good to laugh again. "What about *your* heart?" Matthew said. "Do you think I don't know that you're sweet on Mary Ann?"

Joseph came up scrambling. "What?" he said. "That cocky little hen? She thinks she knows everything."

"Maybe she does, too. I know she thinks you're a great hero. You *defended* her."

Joseph slugged Matthew on the shoulder, but he was trying not to laugh. "Well, I'm not sweet on her," he said. "And don't ever say that again."

Matthew picked up his ax. "It wouldn't be so bad if you were," he said. "She's not a bad girl, even if she is a little sassy. But you've got plenty of time for that, Joseph. Don't get in a hurry."

"Matthew, I don't even know what you're talking about."

Matthew swung his ax over his shoulder and set his foot against a small log, but he stayed in that position and looked at Joseph again. "Joseph," he said, "I know it's not easy for you not to have a father. It seems to get harder instead of easier, doesn't it?"

Joseph didn't know why Matthew had brought that up now. "I guess so," he said.

"What I mean is, you aren't going to have him to answer any questions for you, and I just haven't tried."

"I guess I understand what I need to," Joseph said. He was embarrassed, and he was not eager to push the conversation any further.

"All right." Matthew brought the ax down hard, as though he were relieved. But Joseph didn't start chopping. Matthew finally looked back at him.

"Matthew, there is something else."

"What is it?" Matthew put his ax down again.

"When I stole that boat—down on the Missouri—I told that man I would pay him for it when I could. But now I don't see how I can. I don't have any money or any way of getting any."

"After what they did to us, Joseph, I just don't think you should worry about it. They took our land and everything we've built up here."

"*He* didn't, Matthew. We can't always just say 'they' and mean everyone who's not one of us. That man didn't care a bit— one way or the other—about Mormons."

"It was an old boat, Joseph. And you saved lives by taking it. You did the right thing. You can't help it."

"But I want to feel right about this whole thing, Matthew."

"I guess I'm over that now, Joseph. We made some mistakes, but we were never what they were. My conscience is clear—and I think yours should be too. But if I can get a couple of dollars somehow, you can try to get them to that old man. I can't promise anything though."

Joseph had to be satisfied with that. There wasn't much more he could do.

Chapter 17

Only a few days later, Brigham Young came to the Williams' home and asked to see Joseph. Joseph walked outside, and the two of them stood in the dooryard. Brigham Young was a strong man with a firm jaw and steady eyes. He took Joseph's upper arm and turned him just a little so that he could look directly into the boy's face. "I understand you lived in Clay County, Joseph."

"Yes, I did, Brother Brigham."

"Can you get there with snow on the ground, maybe covering the road in places?"

"Sure. But I don't have a horse anymore."

"We have a horse you can use. We want you to take a letter to the Prophet. Can you leave in the morning?"

"Yes. Sure." Joseph did not look forward to the cold ride, but he did want to see Joseph Smith.

"All right. I'll bring the letter later today. Leave early, and maybe you can make it in one day. But the days are short now, and it's going to be a long ride in the snow. It's close to thirty miles, isn't it?"

"About that, I think," Joseph said. "I'll find a place to stop for the night if I have to."

"Do that, Joseph, but be careful. It might be better if you don't let anyone know where you're going, or even that you're one of us."

Joseph understood. He and Brother Brigham shook hands. The next morning Joseph left early, before sunup. But the going was slow, and he was not able to make it in one day. He stopped at a house, however, and was taken in for the night. The people were kindly but not talkative, and they didn't ask who he was or whether he was a Mormon, and Joseph didn't volunteer any information. In fact, he noticed himself using his Missouri dialect almost unconsciously.

The next day he made it to the jail fairly early. It was an ugly place from the outside, built of gray stone, and it was not much bigger than a smokehouse. But Joseph was unprepared for what he saw when he went inside. He was allowed to climb down into the cellar. It was dark down there, and at first he could hardly see anything. The smell was disgusting, musty and rotten, and all too much like an outhouse. "Joseph Williams," he heard the Prophet say, and then someone stepped closer in the darkness. But the man hardly looked like Joseph Smith. He was thin and his hair had grown longer than usual. Joseph looked around the room in wonder. The brethren had no beds, just straw and blankets on the stone floor. Only two openings, just narrow slits at the top of the walls, allowed in any light or air. Sidney Rigdon was lying on the floor, apparently asleep. When Joseph looked at him, the Prophet said, "Sidney's not well, Joseph. He's suffered terribly."

Joseph shook hands with the others. Hyrum was glad to see Joseph, but the men were all rather subdued, and they looked weak and thin. When Brother McRae stood up to shake hands with Joseph, he remained stooped, since the ceiling was not as high as his head. Joseph's eyes were becoming more accustomed to the dark, and now he could see the Prophet's face much better. His skin, in the half-light, seemed to have a yellow cast and his eyes looked dark and deep. "Are you all right?" Joseph asked.

"Yes," the Prophet answered. He chuckled. "We're not quite as bad as we look. How do you like our quarters?"

"I don't know how you can stand it."

"A man can stand more than he thinks he can, Joseph. But it hasn't been easy."

Joseph nodded and looked around again. It made him angry to think that any human beings could be treated this way. "I have a letter from Brigham Young for you," he finally said.

"Good. I hoped you would. In a few minutes we'll see if the jailer will let us go up above where I can see better. I want to write a letter to send back. But first I want to hear about what's been happening in Far West. Is everyone all right?" The Prophet leaned against the wall.

"Well, there's been an awful lot of illness, Brother Joseph. I guess you know about that. Did anyone tell you that David Osborne's baby died?"

"Yes, we heard that some time ago. There haven't been any lately, I hope."

"Not that I know of. But a lot of people are starting to move out now, and that's making room for more to move inside. I did want to tell you that I saw Sister Emma the day before yesterday, and she looked fine." Joseph looked across the room. "And Brother Hyrum, I saw your new son. He's a fine looking boy— with a good name."

"You mean Fielding?" Hyrum said good-naturedly.

"Well, no. I meant the Joseph part."

"Tell me more about Emma," Joseph Smith said. "Was she in good spirits?"

"Not bad, Brother Joseph. Not too bad—if you consider everything. She told my mother how much your letters help her."

"That's good. I'm glad to hear that. What about my children? Do you ever see them?"

"Well, not the baby. But I sometimes see little Joseph out playing by your house. He looks well enough—and he's growing. He's going to be taller than you, I'd say."

Joseph Smith nodded.

"Don't they ever let you out of here?" Joseph asked.

"Sometimes. The jailer's not a bad man—at least now that he's gotten to know us a little. When he can, he takes us out for a walk. We've taken our share of abuse, though. Some of the others have . . . well, let's not talk about that now. Tell me about yourself, Joseph. Are you getting to be religious?"

Joseph knew that he was getting teased, but the question struck him as a rather interesting one. Joseph *had* felt differently about church meetings lately. Once most of the soldiers had cleared out of Far West, services had been held again, and Joseph had listened as he never had before. "I guess I am," he said. "At least I've been giving some things more serious thought than I used to."

The Prophet sensed his seriousness. "Let's sit down," he said. There were some stools that Joseph Smith pulled over. "What's happened to you, Joseph? Are you growing up?"

"I don't know. I guess it's about time. I'll be seventeen before too long."

"Seventeen. Joseph, there's been plenty asked of you for a boy your age. I guess you *would* start to ask some serious questions." The Prophet stretched his legs out in front of him, and he leaned back on the stool as best he could. "What kinds of things have you been thinking about?"

Joseph felt self-conscious. He knew all the other men could hear him. He wished he could be alone with Joseph Smith. And yet he didn't want to miss this opportunity. He had been wanting to talk with the Prophet. "Well, it's not easy to say." Joseph had never put his concerns into words, and he struggled to find language for them now. "I went to Haun's Mill and saw what happened there. I've never seen things like that before."

"Joseph," the Prophet said, "it's something we all have to discover sooner or later. I thought maybe you knew. I thought you had seen what people can be—back in Jackson County."

"It was different then."

"How was it different?"

Joseph thought about it. "I don't know. Back then I never thought of the old settlers as being like us. They were the enemy."

"Wasn't that the case in Caldwell County?

Joseph sat quietly for a time. "Brother Joseph," he said eventually, "I know about the Danites."

Joseph Smith nodded, and then he held his head down. "And so now you ask yourself if we are any better than the enemy. Is that it?"

"Matthew says they were worse than us—and I guess that's right. I mean, I understand that we were fighting back. But . . .'"

"But what, Joseph?"

Joseph was feeling the pain of it all, now that he was dredging everything back up. "I don't know, Brother Joseph. I just thought the Saints wouldn't ever do such things."

The Prophet let Joseph think for a time, and then he said, "Joseph, those men who murdered our people at Haun's Mill— what do you suppose they did when they got home?"

"I'm not sure what you mean."

"Do you think they go about killing people all the time?"

"No."

"That's right, Joseph. They went back to their homes, back to their children and wives, farmed their land, went on about the same as we do. Wouldn't you guess that's right?"

Joseph nodded, and yet the idea was somehow astounding to him.

The Prophet asked, "Do you think they all *look* like murderers?"

"I guess not."

"Do you see what I'm getting at, Joseph? Evil is not something done by a select little group of people. Men who seem very kind in one situation can do horrifying things in another."

"I know that, Brother Joseph. I guess I've understood that much for a long time. But I didn't think any of our own people would go so far."

"Not many of them did, Joseph. But the important thing you need to realize is that *every* person is capable of the kind of sin you've seen these last few months."

"You aren't, Brother Joseph. My father wasn't."

"But that's where you're wrong. *Everyone* is capable of evil. Don't you think *you* are?"

"Not like that. I couldn't kill someone—not just stand there and shoot some little boy's head off."

The Prophet stood up and stepped directly in front of Joseph. He leaned forward. "Joseph, listen to me. I don't think you ever *would* do such a thing. But it is very important that you recognize that you *could* do it. You want the enemy always to be some evil spirit fighting on the other side, but that's a child's view. The real enemy is within you, Joseph. It's the most important thing you can learn in this world."

"Then what's the difference?" Joseph said, and his voice showed his frustration. "If we're just as evil as everyone else, what are we—"

"No, Joseph. I didn't say that. I said we were *capable* of the same evil. But there is a difference. Some of our people gave in to their passion for revenge, but most of us never let go. Sometimes we wanted to, but we didn't." Joseph thought about that, but he didn't respond. "All people are weak. It's in our nature, Joseph. We're petty and greedy, and we're terribly selfish. Look within yourself if you don't believe it. But people who triumph are the ones who struggle all their lives to resist their own weakness. A lot of those old settlers just let go—quit resisting—and so did some of our people. But the ones who won out were the ones who didn't. Think of Alexander Doniphan. He put himself in great danger when he refused to shoot me."

"But just because not as many of our people—"

"No, Joseph, you're not listening to me. The victors are the people on both sides who never gave in to their animal passions. And I'm telling you that as a people, we came out pretty well. We triumphed. We're still going to build our city—somewhere. And we can do it, because those of us who are going on are stronger than we ever were. We've taken on a terrible enemy— ourselves—and we didn't lose."

Somehow this all seemed like "funeral talk" to Joseph. He wanted to believe the Prophet, to accept his way of seeing things—but all he said seemed to describe so little of what Joseph had actually seen. "Did you know about the Danites, Brother Joseph?"

Joseph Smith sat back down. "Is that one of the things you've been worried about?"

"Yes."

"I knew they existed. But I didn't know what kinds of things they started to do at the last. I didn't know what Avard was telling them to do. I know that sounds hollow, but it's true."

"But why didn't you know?"

The Prophet sat quietly. Joseph knew that everyone in the room was listening, except for Sidney Rigdon, who was still sleeping, breathing with difficulty. "I've had plenty of time to think about my mistakes," Joseph Smith said. "I *should* have known. You're right about that. But I think I was caught up in my own pride at the time. I thought we could fight *any* army and win. I thought it was our destiny. This jail has been good for me, Joseph. I understand God's purposes better than I ever have before."

Joseph didn't respond at first, and the Prophet waited. Joseph felt he had to say something, but he still felt a gnawing sense that he was not quite satisfied. "I need to think about all this," he said.

"Do that, Joseph. And look within yourself. You're old enough now to begin to understand, to be honest with yourself about your own capabilities—both for good *and* evil."

"There *is* one thing I feel guilty about," Joseph said. "I owe that man for his boat—the one I stole. And I don't have any money to pay him with."

"How much do you owe him?"

"Matthew thinks a couple of dollars would be enough."

"I'll give you three, Joseph. You go pay him. You can pay me back later. You clear your conscience of that and then look within yourself again." He put his hand on the boy's shoulder. "Joseph, your mission has begun. You served your people well in Caldwell County. You completed every task you were given—courageously. But there are bigger things ahead for you. You need to be ready for them. You need to find out what's inside you.

And you don't need to be frightened to find out you're human. It's our very weakness that makes goodness a kind of miracle."

Joseph listened. And he accepted the money Joseph Smith gave him. But he didn't really understand what the Prophet wanted from him. He knew he was weak; he knew that all too well. But what did that have to do with murdering children and driving families from their homes?

He waited while the Prophet wrote a letter to Brigham Young, and one to Emma, and then he left. He was not heading home, however; he followed the river to the east. The first thing he wanted to do was repay the ferryman.

Joseph found the shack without any trouble, and when he approached the door he felt satisfied, even though the ride had taken him far out of his way. He wanted to feel good inside, relieved of this one guilt.

He knocked at the door, and the same old man opened it. "You wanting to cross?" he said. He didn't recognize Joseph.

"No, sir. I came to pay you the money I owe you. I'm the one that took your boat."

"What?" The old man squinted, his eyes straining to see through the film that covered them.

"I stole your boat. Last October. I told you I'd pay for it. I have three dollars for you."

"Let's have it," the old man said.

Joseph took the silver dollars from his pocket and handed them to the man, who was holding out his hand. He rubbed his cracked and dirty thumb over them a time or two. "Did you want to cross?" he said.

"No."

"All right." And then he shut the door.

Joseph stood there, not moving toward his horse. He was amazed. He had expected the man to be surprised, to thank him, to be impressed. He knew that it was only what he owed him, but he still expected some sign of appreciation.

Joseph left, feeling unsatisfied and confused. He had to stop for another night, and he didn't get home until the next day. He had plenty of time to think along the way, but he never really organized his ideas clearly. The one nagging feeling that returned time and again was that his conscience was still not clear. It was as though he owed the man something more—but he couldn't even begin to say what it was.

Chapter 18

The Engberts and Jensons decided to leave Missouri before the end of February. The weather had not been too bad lately and they wanted to cross the state before the spring thaw turned everything into mud. Matthew thought this was wise, but Mother wanted to wait to move until Samuel was doing a little better. And anyway, they didn't have a team. Brigham Young promised that he would get one for them before March was gone.

When the Engberts left, Mother went out and said good-bye and gave Sister Engbert a hug. They had never become terribly close, but they had shared the load through the winter, and they obviously felt that attachment. Joseph walked out too, but he really didn't say anything, just sort of stood back and watched as Matthew helped Brother Engbert get some last things in the wagon. When Mary Ann walked over to him, he was embarrassed. He was afraid Matthew would notice.

"Well, good-bye," she said.

"Good-bye," Joseph said. "I guess we'll see all of you over in Illinois before too long."

"Are you going to miss me, Joseph?" Mary Ann said, with that quick smile of hers, and her eyes full of playfulness.

Joseph couldn't think what to say. He knew she was teasing him, but he was embarrassed anyway. What a thing for her to say. "I'll get by," he finally answered, but he was looking away from her.

And then, before he knew it, she had kissed him on the cheek. The two sisters, and even Ruth, had seen it, and they were all standing together laughing. Joseph stepped back abruptly and felt his ears grow warm. He still wouldn't look at her. What kind of girl would do such a thing? Mother would be shocked if she found out. But as the wagon rolled away, Joseph got a look at her, waving and still enjoying her success. She did look sort of pretty. He had to admit that to himself.

* * *

It was past the middle of March when the Williamses finally left Far West. They had hoped to leave a little earlier, but Samuel hadn't improved much. The first two days of travel were not bad, because Matthew pushed on to the stations that the brethren had set up along the way. Shelters were available at those stops, and usually some firewood. Matthew had convinced the family to leave most of their things behind so that Mother and the little ones could ride and so the mules would not be overly taxed. But it had not been an easy decision for Matthew. Joseph had watched him for two days, and his solemn look had hardly altered. The great weight of starting over again—with nothing—was resting on Matthew more than on anyone else, and he was getting himself ready, solidifying his resolve.

On the third day, the weather turned cold again, and a driving snow fell all morning. Matthew kept the mules going as long as he could, but he had to let them stop before they reached the station that night. It was a bad night, with the wind howling in the trees around them, and filling the wagon with painful cold. The snow had stopped, but it was drifting now.

All day Samuel had continued to cough, and when he tried to sleep that night, the cough only got worse. By midnight he was coughing violently, even spitting up blood. Joseph and Matthew were under the wagon, wrapped in blankets, but they were miserably cold. Joseph couldn't sleep at all. He lay there and listened to his little brother's choking coughs. Matthew finally got up and tried to start a fire, telling Joseph that maybe some herb tea would help Samuel. Joseph got up with him, and they huddled over a little scrap of scorched cloth while Matthew chipped away with his flint and steel. The cloth would start, but there was not enough dry grass to get much of anything going. They finally gave up, wrapped themselves back up in their blankets and waited for morning, not even thinking of sleep.

Toward morning, as the sun was just starting to lighten the sky, Joseph heard a new sound, muffled and just discernible. Then he realized that it was someone crying. It was Mother. Samuel had never stopped coughing, and Joseph thought maybe Mother was feeling concern and fatigue, but when he got up and asked, she said that Ruth was getting sick, that she had taken a fever and was already very hot.

That morning Matthew got out and led the mules, pulling them through the drifts. They made it to the station in the early afternoon, stopped, and got the children inside. But the little log shelter had no fireplace. It was warmer than the wagon but still very cold. Matthew did manage to build a fire outside, and they ate a better meal that night, but Samuel was getting worse, coughing until he was drained of all strength. And Ruth's fever was raging. She vomited almost everything she tried to eat.

The next day was somewhat warmer. Matthew decided it

was better to push ahead than to stay in conditions that simply weren't that much better than those in the wagon. He thought their best hope was to make it to the Mississippi as fast as they could. Once they crossed the river, they would find other Saints who could help them.

But by mid-morning the snow was beginning to melt, and the mules struggled to get footing in the slush and melting ice. As the sun was going down that afternoon, they were far from the next station, with no hope of reaching it that day. Samuel was not coughing so much, but he was very weak. Mother said it would be better if he did cough. She could hear the gurgling sound in his chest. Joseph knew what that meant. Samuel's eyes, brown like Matthew's, had lost almost all life, and his skin was thin and blue. He didn't even seem to recognize anyone.

Joseph had been trying to decide what to do. Eventually he said, "Matthew, I think we'd better try to get Samuel and Ruth inside tonight. The way the sky's clearing off, it's going to be awfully cold."

"I know. I've been thinking about it." Matthew's eyes were trained on the road ahead. "We're going to have to stop at the next cabin we see and ask for help. I can't think what else to do."

But there were not many settlers in upper Missouri. When Mathew finally spotted an inhabited cabin, the sun was setting. The cabin was large for this part of the state, and there was a fire burning. Matthew got down from the wagon, and Joseph went with him. Matthew knocked.

A man opened the door, a neat-looking man with a full gray beard and a balding head. "What is it?" he said. He had an accent, maybe German.

"Excuse me, sir, but we have a serious problem. Our little brother is sick—very sick—and so is our sister. We need to get

143

them inside for the night, and we wondered if maybe you could—"

"Who are you?" the man asked, sounding wary, not friendly.

"My name is Matthew Williams, and this is my—"

"Where you coming from?"

Matthew hesitated. "Caldwell County," he said.

"That's what I thought. Mormons. We want nothing to do with you here." He began to close the door.

"Sir." The man left the door open just a crack. "I'm afraid our brother's going to die. He's just a little boy, five years old. And our sister's just ten. If you could let them in, it might save their lives."

"Listen to me," the man said, and the door opened a little wider again. "You've brought this on yourselves. You were the ones who tried to push everyone else out and take everything for yourselves. Now you're paying for it. I don't need your sickness in my house—to share with my family. You move on."

Joseph couldn't stand it. "But they're just little children. Couldn't you just—" The man shut the door.

The boys stood there for a moment, and then they walked back to the wagon. Joseph was angry—burning to tell the man what he thought of him, to make him listen. "What'll we do?" he said.

Matthew didn't answer. He walked to the back of the wagon and looked in. Ruth was lying on her back, apparently asleep, but quietly moaning and letting her head roll back and forth. Mother was holding Samuel. His eyes were half shut and glazed. His arms were hanging down. Mother's hair had fallen down over her shoulders. She looked old, older than she had ever looked before.

"They won't help us," Matthew said. "We'll have to push on and see if there's another house up ahead."

Joseph saw tears come into Mother's eyes. "Then let's push ahead. But we need to hurry, Matthew. He's . . . very low."

Joseph's anger was suddenly more than he could contain. He had to do something. He couldn't just let this happen. He walked to the front of the wagon, not quickly, not drawing Matthew's attention. There was a corn-knife in the front of the wagon, the closest thing to a weapon they had. Joseph grabbed it and walked a few steps toward the house, his mind very clear about what he was going to do. He ran the last steps and threw himself against the door. It was not barred, and it gave way easily. Joseph was in the room. He was holding the knife in front of him.

The man had been sitting with his wife by the fire. There were others in the room, some children, but Joseph didn't look around. He stared at the man, who stood up. "You can't do this to them," Joseph said. "You're killing little children. You're not even human."

The man was stunned. He said nothing. Joseph saw the woman now, still sitting, looking wholesome and warm by the fire, but terribly shocked. They didn't look as evil as Joseph wanted them to look.

"Young man, you can't—"

"Yes, I can. I'm bringing my brother and sister in here, and you're letting them sleep here tonight. I'll stab you if I have to!" He heard someone in the room let out a little shriek. In fact, the sound had come and gone several times since he had first burst through the door, but he had not listened before.

The man walked slowly forward, toward Joseph. "Give me that knife," he said. Joseph took a step back.

"Don't, I'll stab you! I will!" He gestured with the knife, plunging it forward.

"Joseph, no!" It was Matthew, at the door. Joseph didn't look at him.

The man was close now, close enough to stab. Joseph wanted to do it. He wanted to drive the knife into the man's chest—before it was too late. "Give it to me," the man said.

Joseph stepped back again. He raised the knife above his shoulder, gripped it tight. He couldn't let this man keep coming forward. He couldn't let him take another step. "You can't just murder them," he said. "They're human beings. And so are you." He was crying now, and he knew it was too late. The man stepped forward again, and Joseph let the knife fall to his side. Matthew came to him and took the knife away. "You can't just sit by the fire and let them die," Joseph said, and he was sobbing. "It's not human."

"Joseph, we don't do things this way," Matthew said.

Joseph was holding his hands over his face. He was already sick with himself. The man put his hand on Joseph's shoulder. This was too much for Joseph. He ran from the house, but when he reached the wagon, he didn't know where to go. He grabbed the side of the wagon and gripped it tight and let himself cry openly. "What is it?" he heard Mother say, but he didn't answer.

In a few seconds she was out of the wagon, standing next to him. She held him around the shoulders. "What happened?" she said.

"I tried to kill him," Joseph said. He gripped the wagon and felt the anguish sweep over him. "I tried to kill that man. I *wanted* to kill him."

"But you didn't, Joseph. You could *never* do that."

Joseph twisted out of her arms and stood looking at her. "Yes I could, Mother. I almost did."

Suddenly Sister Williams grabbed Joseph by the shoulders. "Stop this!" she said, sternly and forcefully. "Joseph, we have no time for this. Stop your crying. We have to push on. We need to get the children inside somewhere."

Joseph was stunned by her firmness. "All right," he said, nodding. "I'll get Matthew."

But Matthew had come up behind them. "It's all right now. We can take the children in."

Mother hurried to the back of the wagon. Joseph stood where he was, not knowing what to do. He couldn't just walk into that man's house—not after what he had done. He leaned against the wagon and watched as Mother and Matthew carried the little ones into the house. He was trying to think what this all meant, trying to understand who he was. Beyond the house the western clouds were glazed in orange. It seemed unreasonable to think that the sun would simply go down as it always had before, and then rise again in the morning.

But then the man came out of the house. He walked to Joseph and put his hand on his shoulder again. "Come into my house," he said. "I *am* human—and so are you."

Chapter 19

Samuel died. Not that night, but two nights later. The Williamses had been allowed to stay, and the woman, Mrs. Schmidt, had been very kind. But Samuel was just too weak. Ruth, however, gradually got better.

Mr. Schmidt helped the boys dig a grave in the woods across the road from his farm. The Schmidts, with all six of their children, went to the woods with Matthew and Joseph and Sister Williams. Ruth was still in bed. Mr. Schmidt had built a box for a casket.

The day was fairly warm, with only a thin sheet of clouds to diffuse the directness of the sun. It was muddy in the woods, and the wind was jerking the treetops about. Joseph would always remember it as an ugly day full of pain.

Joseph and Matthew put the box down in the grave, and then Matthew said the prayer. He praised God for his mercy in letting Ruth survive. It was difficult for Joseph to feel much sense of mercy, but he believed it was right, and respected Matthew for saying it. "Keep little Samuel until we can all be together again," Matthew said. Joseph could hardly stand to listen. Matthew could say no more. But he never cried. He was like steel now. He was going to preserve what he could of his family, whatever it took. Mother had lost some of her strength, at least for the present, and Joseph could see that Matthew was bringing himself up, preparing for the hard days ahead.

Mother cried, but she never really let go. She was willing herself to survive. Joseph could see it in her face, which was full of pain, but not capitulation.

* * *

The Schmidts kept the Williams family in their home until Ruth was completely recovered, not just for a few nights, but for almost four weeks. Mr. Schmidt was ashamed that he had at first tried to turn them away; he wanted to go to all lengths to correct the first impression he had made. "You cannot imagine what things were said about your people," he told Matthew and Joseph. "We thought you were all monsters." Matthew said that he understood, that all too often the Mormons had talked the same way about the old settlers in Missouri.

When Ruth was ready to travel, the family set out again, now only the four of them. Mother looked thin but Joseph could see that she was going to be all right. She was a stronger woman than when she had arrived with the first Saints in Jackson County. She had been an eastern woman then, but now she looked as tough and resolute as any frontier woman. There was no talk of going back to New York, no regrets that they had come to Missouri. Joseph knew that she had resolved those feelings now.

It was Ruth who had lost the most, who had the most to recover. She didn't understand the things that had happened to them, and she was confused and quiet. She sat in the wagon as they traveled, usually looking out the back, rarely speaking.

They reached the Mississippi on the third day. It was a nice

149

April morning when they reached the riverbank. But they had to wait until afternoon for the ferry. Joseph spent his time watching the river, thinking about his years in Missouri, still looking inside himself as Joseph Smith had told him to do. Since the night Joseph had threatened the Schmidts with the corn-knife, he had hardly been the same person, or at least he didn't seem so to himself.

When the ferry eventually arrived, some of the men getting off were familiar: Brigham Young and Heber Kimball, and some of the other apostles. The men came to the Williamses when they saw them, greeted them warmly, and they brought good news: Joseph Smith and the other brethren had been released and were free and safe. Guards had actually let them escape while moving them to another jail.

"But where are you going?" Matthew asked.

"Back to Far West," Brigham Young said. He smiled just a little, as though he expected Matthew to be surprised.

"But why? Won't you be in danger?"

He nodded, but the expression on his face didn't change. "We'll be all right," he said. "Last year—I guess you might remember—Joseph Smith prophesied that we apostles would leave on a mission on April twenty-sixth. He said we'd depart from the temple site in Far West. Some of the old Missourians have been saying that they're sure that's one prophecy that won't come to pass. But we're going back to see to it that it does."

"But Brother Brigham," Joseph said, "I don't see how you can leave the Saints now."

"The work is not going to stop," Brigham Young said. "We have to show our enemies that we aren't going to be defeated that easily."

Joseph hadn't expected this. He looked at these men, all looking strong and confident. He had expected to find a vanquished people in Illinois. He had hoped only for a slow recovery at best.

"We're going to be stronger than ever," Heber Kimball said.

Brigham Young nodded and said, "That's right," and then he shook his fist. There was no sign of anger in the motion, but there was resolve, and there was strength. Joseph believed him. He thought of what Joseph Smith had said, that the Saints would turn their defeat into triumph. It had seemed so unlikely then, in the confines of the miserable Liberty jail.

The brethren talked to Sister Williams for a few minutes, trying to console her about Samuel, and they gave her what news they could of the Saints already in Illinois. But then they had to hurry on. When Matthew drove the wagon onto the ferry, the apostles were riding off on their horses, heading back to Far West.

Joseph got down from the wagon and walked to the back of the ferry. He watched the brethren ride away. And after they were out of sight, he watched the green hills of Missouri slide into the distance. Ruth came back and stood next to him. "Can you remember when we came up the Missouri on that old riverboat?" Joseph asked her.

Ruth shook her head. "No," she said, "I was just little then."

"Matthew and I weren't very big ourselves," he said, and he smiled when he thought of those excited little boys, anxious about their adventure. "Ruth, are you all right?"

"I guess so," she said. Her light hair was pretty in the sun, but she looked thin, and not as strong as Mother. "I miss our house. And I miss Samuel."

"So do I," Joseph said, nodding. "And I miss Father. Do you remember him, Ruth?"

"A little."

Joseph and she looked out across the water again. "Listen,

Ruth," Joseph said. "Don't worry. We'll be fine. We'll find a place, and we'll build us a new home."

"Won't people just take it away again?"

It was the terrible question, the one Joseph hated most to ask. He hardly knew what to say. "Well, I guess it *could* happen again. I don't know."

Joseph watched her, trying to think of something to say that might help. She wouldn't look at him. "It's not fair," she finally said.

Joseph looked where she was looking, at the green hills. He felt the overpowering justice of her words. "I know," he said. He put his arm around her shoulders. "That's what I've been saying for all these years, Ruth. But it really doesn't help much to look at it that way." He tried hard to think of the right words, to make clear what he was beginning to see. "I've been angry ever since those men first gave Father that terrible beating. Back then I just thought we needed to get away from all the bad people so everything would be all right. But it's not like that, Ruth. *Things* aren't just fair or unfair—people are the ones who . . ."

Joseph stopped. He was saying it all wrong. How could he possibly give her, in a few words, what he had gone through so much to learn? "Ruth, houses don't really matter. But the *city* matters—the city we keep trying to build. Do you understand what I'm saying?"

She didn't look up. She shrugged her shoulders. "I don't know for sure."

Joseph thought back to the day on the prairie when he had found the woman who had been driven from her home. He thought of the little baby she had nursed. He thought of Joseph Smith in the Liberty Jail, telling him to look inside himself, telling him that his mission had begun. He thought of himself

152

with the knife, facing what he thought was his enemy. He tried to find among these experiences the words he needed.

Joseph turned Ruth toward himself, holding her by the shoulders. He bent and looked into her eyes. He was struck again with her face, so much like his own. Her eyes were a little darker, but also blue, and also brooding with questions. "Ruth, you'll understand more—in time. I'm sure you will. And I'll try to explain what I know as well as I can. But let's not think so much about what's just happened, all right? I have to fight all the time not to do that. I have to think about what we're going to do next. We're going to build the city, and I'm going to help. You're big enough to help too."

She nodded, but she resisted looking at him very long. She turned back toward the Missouri side of the river. Joseph decided not to push her anymore right then. There would be plenty of time to talk later on. And for now Joseph was rather caught up in his own vision of the future. He knew what Joseph Smith had said was true. His mission *had* begun. He would not only help *build* the city, but he would enter it and be part of it, more than he ever had before.

In a few minutes Matthew came up behind them. "You two have looked back long enough," he said. "Let's do this the right way—the way we've done it before." And so the boys and Ruth went and got Mother from the wagon, and the four of them walked to the front of the ferry. They watched the Illinois shore gradually draw closer. The hills were green and beautiful on that side of the river as well.